/10

I love

isting

e out

/11

/12

8/13

. And

ιts encouraging to read books—especially Viking Quest novels—
that stress family relationships. Most inspiring was that of Bree
and Devin. Closeness between siblings is something that is missing from many homes today. Keep up the family values!"

——**Ben**, 17, Minnesota

"I wanted to write and tell you how much I enjoyed *Raiders from the
Sea*, the first Viking Quest book. I know it says on the back that
the book is for ages ten and up. But I, as a 19-year-old, loved it!
Thank you for writing wholesome books and having Christian
young people (Bree and Devin and others) show what it means to
live a life of faith and trust in God."

——**Rachel**, 19, Minnesota

"I just finished the first two books of the Viking Quest series. M
mother's family is from Norway and my father's family is Scottish,
Irish, and English so I have a great love of any Celtic or Scan-
dinavian based book . . . Thank you so much for the work you are
doing in making GOOD, well written, Christian books available
to young people. I can't wait till I get my sister hooked!!!"

——**Hannah**, 14, Missouri

"I just finished reading the three books in the Viking Quest series. I bought them for my nine-year-old son, but couldn't put them down myself! I started reading *Raiders of the Sea* to my boys yesterday (ages 9 and 5). They protested profusely when I told them we had to stop so they could go to bed. When I got up this morning, my 9-year-old son was on the couch reading. It really is a page turner."

—**Donna Meier,** Connecticut

"I just wanted to let you know your new Viking series is amazing! I've never been into reading, but for some reason or another, your books capture me and I finish them within a couple days! Thank you for what you do."

—**Megan,** 19, Minnesota

"I love your Viking books! When our family reads them aloud together, even our dog listens."

—**Brittany,** 14, Minnesota

"I have ordered the book already from CBD (That is how much I can't wait until February!!!!). I love your books and Web site!!!!!"

—**Lyndsey,** 15, Ohio

"We received *The Invisible Friend* today in the mail. I sat down and read it all the way through without stopping. Wow, I am ready for Book #4! Tonight we will start reading these books together as a family. God has blessed you with a wonderful ability to communicate the gospel through writing."

—**Judy Carter,** Missouri

VIKING ✦ QUEST | book four

ɧEART
of
COURAGE

LOIS WALFRID JOHNSON

MOODY PUBLISHERS
CHICAGO

© 2005 by
LOIS WALFRID JOHNSON

King Olaf Tryggvason, Bjarni Herjulfsson, Erik the Red, his wife Thjodhild, and their sons, Leif, Thorstein, and Thorvald, lived in the time period of this novel. Other characters are fictitious and spring with gratitude for life from the author's imagination. Any resemblance to people living or dead is coincidental. The area called Nidaros is now Trondheim, Norway, and the settlement surrounded by seven mountains is Bergen. Reykjanes is now called Reykjavik. The site of the historic *Althing* in the year 1000 is Thingvellir, presently a national park a short distance from Reykjavik, Iceland.

All Scripture quotations, unless otherwise indicated, are taken from the *Holy Bible, New Living Translation*, copyright © 1996. Used by permission of Tyndale House Publishers, Inc., Wheaton Illinois 60189, U.S.A. All rights reserved.

Isaiah 43:1-3; Matthew 14:27

Published in association with the literary agency of Alive Communications, Inc., 7680 Goddard Street, Suite 200, Colorado Springs, Colorado 80920.

ISBN: 0-8024-3115-1
EAN/ISBN-13: 978-0-8024-3115-8

Library of Congress Cataloging-in-Publication Data

Johnson, Lois Walfrid.
    Heart of courage / Lois Walfrid Johnson.
        p. cm. — (Viking quest ; bk. 4)
    Summary: In the tenth century, as Devin, Keely, and Lil return to Ireland, Bree serves as Mikkel's cook on a voyage in the North Atlantic, but acts of sabotage threaten Mikkel's life and Bree's one chance of freedom.
    ISBN 0-8024-3115-1
        1. Vikings—Juvenile fiction. [1. Vikings—Fiction. 2. Explorers—Fiction. 3. Slaves—Fiction. 4. Christian life—Fiction. 5. Sea stories.] I. Title.

PZ7.J63255He 2005
[Fic]--dc22

                                                            2004022965

1 3 5 7 9 10 8 6 4 2

Printed in the United States of America

To
Daniel, Nate, and Justin
with love and gratitude
for your courageous hearts

CONTENTS

INTRODUCTION

To each of us there usually comes at least one time when we face something so difficult that we wonder if we can do what is needed. Yet if we make the right choices at the right time, we one day look back and realize that we received a very special gift. God be with you, my friend, as you gain a heart of courage.

THE WARNING

When Briana O'Toole heard the sound, she was still partly asleep. *What is it?* she wondered. The noise seemed near and yet far away. What had wakened her in the darkness before dawn?

Through an open door in the barn where she slept, Bree heard fishermen load bait and tackle. Next came a scrape across the shore as they slid their boats into the Norwegian fjord. A moment later, oars creaked as men from the village of Aurland rowed away for their daily catch.

By now, on that early summer morning late in the tenth century, the sounds were familiar to Bree. *Why do such everyday noises make me afraid?*

Then Bree knew. Only last night her brother Devin had told her that he might leave for Ireland soon. Like a warning deep inside, Bree felt sure that on this day she would learn more. No doubt it would be something she must face, like it or not.

High in the hayloft where she slept, Bree pushed back her blanket. On her first night of serving Mikkel's family, she had made her own soft bed—a nest of fragrant hay gathered from a mountainside. By now nine months had passed since the Viking raid that brought Bree and other Irish captives to this village.

In spite of all that had happened, Bree smiled, for she knew something that only the Irish knew. No one else. Not Mikkel, the fifteen-year-old leader of the raid that took Bree away. Not his father, Sigurd, chieftain of the Aurland Fjord. Not his mother Rika. Nor his brother Cort. Nor his grandparents.

My daddy is an Irish chieftain, Bree thought. *A wise and powerful chieftain who cares about his people.* Though she appeared to be a slave, Bree held the secret knowledge of being deeply loved. She felt freedom in her heart.

Reaching out in the darkness, Bree picked up her clothing and quickly dressed. As she pulled on her shoes, she heard a sea chest being dropped heavily into a ship, then footsteps coming up the path from the fjord.

With swift movements, Bree grabbed a rung and scrambled down the ladder. Through the dark barn she hurried, so familiar now with its turns that she needed no light. When she opened the door that connected the barn and the house, she heard Mikkel's angry voice.

"I can't!" he exclaimed. "I won't!"

Without making a sound, Bree entered the hallway that led to the large room where the family ate, slept, and talked. Then the door creaked shut and the room grew instantly silent.

It made Bree uncomfortable. *What were they saying about me?* The question pounded at her heart.

Acting as if she hadn't noticed anything unusual, Bree hurried to the long open hearth. As she stirred the embers, the fire flared, and she added more wood. Taking a large wooden spoon, she stirred the porridge. By the time a knock came on the outer door, she was ready.

When Mikkel swung the door wide, Ingmar stood outside. Taller than Mikkel and with darker blond hair, Ingmar was at least four years older. He was also master of the ship that had given safe passage to Bree's brother Devin when he sailed from Ireland to the Norwegian fjord.

Seeing Ingmar, Mikkel stepped back, as though not wanting to talk with him. Only recently the *ting*, the assembly of freemen, had settled Devin's future and the argument between Ingmar and Mikkel.

Now Ingmar's quick glance went to Bree, then back to Mikkel. Suddenly Ingmar stretched out his hand. "Our freemen have spoken," he said. "By their vote, they freed Bree's brother, Devin."

Looking down at Ingmar's hand, Mikkel stiffened, but Ingmar went on. "You and I are blood cousins, Mikkel. Let's be friends."

For an instant Mikkel glanced toward his father Sigurd. The chieftain sat on a bench along the wall as though waiting to see what would happen. Turning back, Mikkel faced Ingmar again.

With one swift movement, Mikkel pushed aside his flyaway hair. Then, as though making a deliberate choice, he stretched out his hand and shook Ingmar's.

A look of relief filled the young man's eyes. "We finish loading my ship today," Ingmar said. "If the wind blows fair tomorrow, we will leave."

Mikkel nodded, waiting.

"I'll take Bree's brother with me." Though Ingmar spoke to the family, he watched Bree. "I'll take her sister Keely and friend Lil. I'll bring them safely to Dublin."

Without warning, Bree's eyes filled with tears. *It's here. The moment I dreaded.*

But then she understood. Ingmar had come to warn her, to give her one last day to say good-bye. As a tight knot formed in Bree's stomach, she recognized his gift. *No more snatching your family away,* Ingmar was saying without words. *I'm doing my best to help you.*

Slowly Bree put down the large wooden spoon. Her

head high, she stepped out from behind the large cooking pot that hung on a chain from the ceiling. Her shoulders back, she walked around the end of the hearth and stood before Ingmar. With the grace of a young woman before a king, Bree took the edges of her skirt in hand and curtsied low before him.

"I thank you," she said softly.

When she looked up again, Bree saw the kindness in Ingmar's eyes and knew she had rightly understood his wish to help her. Then she saw something more—the courage that molded Ingmar's life to speak to Mikkel as he had.

This time Ingmar spoke directly to her. "When I return to Aurland, I'll tell you. You will know that your brother, sister, and friend are safe in Ireland."

Once more Bree curtsied low. As she straightened, standing tall, Ingmar nodded, accepting her thanks. As he turned away, his face showed his concern for her. When he stepped outside, he closed the door quietly.

As Bree walked back to the fire, no one spoke. When she picked up the large wooden spoon and dished up porridge, no one spoke. But now Bree guessed the meaning of Mikkel's words as she entered the room. She felt sure his mother and father had said, "Set Bree free. Send her back to Ireland with her brother and sister." And Mikkel answered, *"I can't. I won't!"*

If so, it was still another reason for Bree to be angry

with Mikkel. He knew she was a valuable slave, and his greed always won.

When Bree finished serving the family, she dished up her own porridge and took it outside. On the step over-looking the fjord, she sat, quiet and alone. In spite of the ache in her chest and the knot in her stomach, she prom-ised herself that she would make it through.

I can manage, Bree thought, though it tore her apart. But the longer she watched the men load Ingmar's ship, the more difficult it became.

One more day, she told herself. *Tomorrow I'll be alone again.*

Alone. For how long?

Forever?

At the recent assembly where Devin was set free, Bree worked out a way to ransom her sister Keely and friend Lil. Only Bree remained a slave. Then Mikkel offered a startling plan.

"Be my storyteller," he told Devin. "If you and Bree go with me on one voyage, I'll set her free when we return home."

Free! Just the sound of it filled Bree with hope. *No longer a Viking slave!*

"I'm Irish," Devin told Mikkel. "I'm not like your poets."

But Mikkel insisted. "Be my storyteller. Be my friend."

Looking Mikkel straight in the eye, Devin repeated the condition. "If Bree and I go with you for one voyage, you will set her free when we return."

Now, like a sword, fear struck down Bree's courage. Deep inside, she felt a warning she could not ignore. *How good is Mikkel's promise? Can Dev and I trust him to do what's right?*

Courage, Bree thought. *I need courage to help me go beyond the fear I face.*

Just then Mikkel opened the door and came outside. Bree glanced at him and looked away. *If Dev comes back and we sail with Mikkel, will we ever see Ireland again?*

FLIGHT OF THE EAGLE

Mikkel sat down on the wooden step as far from Bree as possible without falling off. Sparks of resentment lit his eyes and flushed his cheeks. After one angry look at Bree, he turned his back to her.

When Mikkel's father, Sigurd, came outside, he walked down the steps between them, turned, and faced them.

Mighty chieftain of the Aurland Fjord, Sigurd had the blue eyes and strong look Mikkel had inherited. With his gray-white hair and beard trimmed short, Sigurd appeared as healthy as when Bree met him nine months before. In the sunlight that shone between the mountains, Bree studied his skin.

Yes! No open sores. No leprosy!

Bree smiled, filled with gladness of heart. Often she had wondered about Sigurd's travels and the terrible disease known in Ireland and many parts of the world. Now Bree wanted to shout, "Wise, kind Sigurd is well!"

Never before, except in the Bible, had Bree heard of someone being healed of leprosy. Yet the chieftain of the Aurland Fjord stood before them, clean.

Closing her eyes, Bree offered a prayer of thanks. As she opened them again, Sigurd's deep voice rumbled with gratitude.

"Thank you, Bree, for telling me about your God."

Bree still felt awed by what God had done. "I'm so glad that He healed you," she said. But Bree knew it was Grandfather who talked most often with Sigurd.

When Bree stole a look at Mikkel, he, too, stared at Sigurd. Even now, Mikkel's gaze traveled over every inch of his father's skin. "It's true!" Mikkel exclaimed, as though it had suddenly sunk in.

Stepping close, Sigurd clapped his son on the shoulder. "Yes, it's really true."

The excitement in Mikkel's face overflowed in his voice. "Even though you stood up in front of everyone, telling all of us—"

"I know," Sigurd said. "It didn't seem real to me either. It still doesn't."

"All those months—"

"Yes. All those months when I kept getting worse—"

All those months when it seemed to Bree that nothing happened. That God wasn't answering Grandfather's prayers, or Rika's, or Dev's, or hers. Then *suddenly*—

"I want to go see our king," Sigurd said now. "He's a Christian, Bree. I want to show him what happened."

"We could sail to Iceland together!" Mikkel exclaimed, as though suddenly realizing the possibilities.

"But first I want to talk with King Olaf," Sigurd said. "I need to speak my gratitude to Bree's God—to tell what He did."

Suddenly Mikkel slouched back against the step. *What's the matter?* Bree wanted to ask. Did Mikkel want his father to be healed without believing in the God who did it?

Sigurd interrupted her thoughts. "Did you tell Bree?"

Mikkel shook his head.

"Why not?" Mikkel's mother Rika spoke from the open doorway behind them.

"At the *ting* I promised that if Devin and Bree sail with me on one voyage, I'll free her when we return home."

In the silence that followed, Bree looked from Sigurd to Rika, then back to Mikkel.

"Bree says her God protects her wherever she goes," he said, looking at his mother.

Rika gasped. "Her God protects her *wherever* she is? Is that true, Bree?"

In that moment Bree remembered her brother's words. "Be careful," Devin had warned. "Mikkel will want you along on a voyage. He'll think that if you're on the ship, he'll be safe."

So. Dev was right. It had happened.

More than anything, Bree did not want to make a false promise to Rika, who had already lost a son to the sea.

"My God—my Jesus—has promised to be with me always," Bree said. "He's promised to protect me. That means if I die, I'll go to be with Him in Heaven."

"You could still die in a storm?" Mikkel was curious now.

"Of course." Bree grinned. "So you don't need me along on your voyage."

"Yes, I do," Mikkel said quickly. "You pray to your God, and I'll pray to mine. That will take care of everything."

But Bree looked at Mikkel's mother. When her husband and sons were gone, Rika saw to every detail of taking care of the house and farm. All day long she made decisions, and she seldom delayed in what she did.

"I've changed my mind," Rika said to Mikkel. "When you go to sea, Bree should cook your meals."

Mikkel's grin spread from ear to ear. But Sigurd had the last word.

"When Mikkel returns from one voyage, he keeps his promise. Bree goes back to her family in Ireland."

Mikkel nodded, his eyes and face solemn. But the minute his father and mother started down to the fjord, Mikkel grinned again.

"So!" Bree's voice was as hard as the iron rivets holding the boards in Mikkel's new ship. "You talked your parents into what you wanted."

Mikkel laughed. "I didn't fool them. My mother liked what I said."

But Bree's anger spilled over. Both Sigurd and Rika were strong-minded people. "They said you should send me home, didn't they?"

At first Bree thought Mikkel wasn't going to answer. "Didn't they?" she asked again.

Without looking at her, he nodded. That made Bree even more angry. "Why don't you let me go? I'm just another Irish your Vikings captured during the raid."

As though it wasn't important, Mikkel shrugged. But to Bree it was life or death, even the air she breathed. "It was your fault that I became a slave."

When Mikkel grew still, Bree knew she had hit a tender spot. "Your own father said you'll never be free until you set things right."

Suddenly Mikkel flared up. "I can't correct what I did. What's more, I don't want to."

Anger burned through his tightly held control. "How

many Irish did my ship bring to Norway? How can I send every one of them back?"

"You can start by sending me home."

"Forget it, Bree. Life is life. You're a slave. That's the way it is."

"No, it's not. I'm not a slave. I never have been. I never will be. No matter how often you call me a slave, I am not."

For a moment she almost told him that she was the daughter of a much-loved Irish chieftain. Instead, bitter words spilled out. "I hate you, hate you, hate you!"

"I know."

Mikkel's quiet words struck Bree more than his anger possibly could. "Why don't you send me off so you don't have to see me again?" she asked.

But Mikkel did not answer. In that moment Bree felt sure that his choice to keep her here was not something she could change, no matter how hard she tried.

Knowing how she would feel when her brother and sister left the next morning, Bree looked toward the Aurland River. A golden eagle soared in the clear air above the mountains. It reminded Bree of the freedom she needed.

"Mikkel, this is the last day I can be with Dev and Keely. Can we climb the mountains together?"

Startled, Mikkel turned to stare at her. "Are you serious?"

"Why not?"

"You'll figure out a way to escape."

"I want a day we can remember."

"No!"

Bree sighed. "I don't want to work all the livelong day."

Instead of answering, Mikkel stood up. Tall and slender, he had surprised Bree more than once with how quickly he moved. Sometimes she wondered if he could run as quickly as the reindeer that roamed the mountaintops. But now Bree knew she was about to lose a day with her brother and sister.

"Come with us, Mikkel."

"Come with you?" he asked.

Bree saw the surprise in his face. "Why not?"

Instead of meeting her eyes, Mikkel looked up at the mountains. Again Bree saw the eagle and wished she could soar just as freely.

Mikkel turned to her. "Bree, I've promised you two things. When the *ting* freed Devin, I asked him to come back after he takes Keely and Lil home. I promised that if both of you go with me on the first voyage in my new ship, I'll give you, Bree, your freedom."

"But how do I know if you'll keep your promise?" she asked.

"When you were taken as a slave, I promised to watch out for you. Have I done it?"

As Bree thought back, she remembered one time after another when Mikkel had kept that promise. Thinking about those dangerous moments, it surprised her. "You have," she said. "And I usually don't thank you, do I?"

Mikkel grinned. "Well, you can start thanking me now by being civil."

"Civil."

"Polite. Not really nice. That would be too much to ask. But not rude."

Civil. Bree thought about it. Usually she was civil to Mikkel only when she had to be. In front of his parents and townspeople, for instance. Because she was a slave for Mikkel's family, they expected her to treat him with a certain level of respect.

"Civil," Bree said again. "All right. I can manage that, even when someone isn't watching."

"And if you *really* want to stretch yourself, you could even be friendly like your brother Devin."

"Oh, no!" Bree exclaimed. "That's going too far. Dev promised that if he comes back from Ireland, he'll be your storyteller and friend. But I'm not willing to be your friend. Not ever. Not in a thousand years."

"All right. I agree." Mikkel grinned again. "Civil. Even when you don't have to because someone is watching."

Bree nodded, but wondered why it seemed important to him. It had never occurred to her to work together with Mikkel. Always Bree had wanted to just get along well enough to get what she wanted.

Now she wondered, *What would happen if I helped him? If I even worked to make his trip a success? Maybe I would be able to go home more quickly!*

"One more thing," she said. "Why don't you show us your favorite place?"

Turning, Mikkel again faced the steep mountains across the Aurland River. "From here it's hard to point out."

Bree was curious now. "Why is it your favorite?"

"When you see it, you'll know."

"You mean we can go?" Bree's delight spilled into her voice.

To her surprise Mikkel nodded. "I'll show you the spot I like more than any other. You fix some food. I'll go for your sister Keely. As soon as I bring her back, we'll get Devin."

Bree couldn't believe it. "Oh, *tusen takk!* A thousand thanks!"

Mikkel looked embarrassed. "Civil, I said. You don't have to overdo it."

Without another word he set out for the farm where Keely had lived for nearly seven years. Bree could hardly believe that Mikkel had given her time with Dev and Keely.

Looking up, Bree saw the eagle again. It soared

directly above her now, where she could see it clearly. *God seems quite good at doing miracles.* With no one but Him to hear, Bree laughed out loud.

THREE

MIKKEL'S TEST

As Bree prepared food, her thoughts were busy elsewhere. *Why do I always want to explore new mountains, lands, and seas?* For as long as she could remember, Bree had wanted to know what lay beyond a turn in the path, a bend in the river, or a clump of trees.

When Mikkel returned with Keely, Bree looked into her sister's eyes and knew they were the same deep brown as her own. But Keely's hair was sandy colored instead of reddish blond and her eyes sparkled with the thought of a trip into the mountains.

With each of them carrying a bundle of food, Mikkel led Keely and Bree to the house where Devin stayed.

"Mikkel said we could hike up the mountain," Keely told her brother as they set out for the river.

Like their father, Devin had the black hair and deep blue eyes of the dark Irish. Now his face seemed lit with excitement.

"Ingmar said you and Keely and Lil are leaving tomorrow," Bree explained.

A startled look entered Devin's eyes. Soon he dropped back to whisper to Bree. "If I come back from Ireland, do you think we can trust Mikkel to let you go?"

"Not if he lets his temper or greed make up his mind." Bree spoke just as softly.

"Or his desire to be famous." There were a lot of things that could get in the way of Mikkel keeping a promise.

"We need to find out," Dev said, and Bree grinned.

Long ago they had discovered ways to learn what they wanted to know about someone who might give them trouble. Who got angry instead of taking something as a joke? Who could they trust to be honest and fair?

With all her heart, Bree wanted her brother's tests to be as difficult as he could make them. Both of them needed to know what Devin should do. What if he returned and lost his freedom again? Or even worse, his life?

Suddenly Bree had a thought. "Do you have any coins left from what the cobbler gave you in Dublin?"

"Just one."

"How would you feel about losing it?"

Devin stared at her. "So I set off from this north country with two young girls and tell myself, 'You can get them back to Ireland without one single coin!'"

When Bree snickered, Devin stopped in his tracks. "Well—maybe for a good cause I could lose it."

As the four of them reached the river, the dog Bree called Shadow caught up. Midsized and black with a curly tail, the dog had become Bree's friend. When she climbed into the small boat, Shadow leaped in also.

Bree and Devin took the oars, and Mikkel took his seat like a king expecting to be served by slaves. They were nearly across the river when Devin lifted the blade of his oar and splashed Mikkel. Water sprayed over his face, shoulder, and sleeve.

"Sorry," Devin said quickly, but the look in Mikkel's eyes told Bree that he guessed the truth. Both Bree and Devin were too good at rowing to splash accidentally.

To Bree's surprise, Mikkel shrugged. "Feels good on a warm day."

On the other side of the river, Shadow raced ahead of them up the steep hill onto a path that rose sharply through a birch wood. When Devin fell into step next to Mikkel, Bree felt curious. What could her brother be saying to Mikkel?

At times they seemed the best of friends. In other

moments Bree caught the anger between them. She felt sure that Dev was digging deep, trying to find out what he wanted to know.

Enemy walking with enemy, Bree decided. How could Mikkel ever be anything else when he had taken so much from them?

Beyond the birch lay a pine wood. Sometimes Shadow raced ahead, chasing a hare. Other times he streaked off into the forest. When he returned, he padded alongside Bree.

"Come here, Shadow," she called, and always he obeyed.

"That's not his name," Mikkel said.

"That's *my* name for him," answered Bree. "He likes to follow me wherever I go."

In the dense pine wood, Bree felt crowded and shut in. When Keely slowed down, Bree wondered if her sister was having trouble with the foot she hurt near the end of winter. Instead Keely said, "I don't want to leave you tomorrow."

"You must." Bree had given her opportunity for freedom to Keely and didn't want her to be sorry later. "Can you imagine how excited Daddy and Mam will be, seeing you again?"

"It doesn't seem real." Keely's smile was soft, but soon disappeared. "You should be the one going. The ransom Dev brought was for you."

In spite of the ache Bree felt, she shook her head. "You need to know your brother and sisters before they're all grown up. Cara and Jen have never even met you!"

Again it worked. Keely smiled. "It's like a dream."

Then as she looked around, the darkness beneath the pine branches seemed to enter her eyes. "Bree, I'll be forever thankful that you gave me your place to go home. But if you don't come back to Ireland, I'll always feel hurt right here." Keely laid her hand over her heart.

Bree laid her own hand on top of Keely's. "I'll come back," Bree promised. "I'll come home."

Just the same, the darkness of the woods filled her spirit. *Will I really go back?* Bree asked herself. She was glad when they reached a more open area.

Sometimes large stones stood like watchmen. Farther on, pine trees grew between stones lying flat on the ground. Where light slanted between the branches, Bree caught glimpses of all that lay below.

The path they climbed switched back and forth, going one way, then another, at an angle up the steep mountainside. Above the tree line Mikkel led them to a deep crevasse in the side of the mountain. The rocks stretched high with only a slender walkway between them.

Like a narrow slit in the earth, there were rough irregular rocks on either side. "Just step where I step," he said.

Again Mikkel went first, reaching out for a handhold, then testing each step. From one narrow ledge to the next he climbed upward. Watching closely, Bree followed, then Keely, and finally Devin.

Higher and higher the trail took them, always turning back on itself. When they rested for a few minutes, Bree looked down on a farm. The house was smaller than the one where Mikkel lived. Yet Bree felt sure that this farmhouse also had the living area at one end and a barn at the other. Beyond that barn Bree saw a large outbuilding.

As Bree watched, a strong looking man of average height came out from the left of the building, walked across the side toward Bree, and disappeared on the right. A moment later he appeared on the left again. When he circled the building a third time Bree felt curious. "That man really walks fast," she said.

Farther up the path, everyone fell silent, as though no one had anything more to say. The deeper the silence grew the more upset Bree felt. Usually she, Devin, and Keely wouldn't be able to talk fast enough. With Mikkel listening to every word, not even Bree could think of something to say.

The next time Mikkel stopped, he stood next to a large flat stone. "Let's eat," he said.

As an uncomfortable silence filled the air between them, Bree set out the food on a clean, flat rock. Dried fish. Thick slices of bread spread with butter. Cheese and small oatcakes made with honey. Shadow dropped down beside Bree and waited for crumbs to fall.

To Bree's surprise Mikkel didn't send the dog away. Instead, he took one look at the food and said, "Thanks, Bree. You brought what I like."

"No, she didn't," Devin said. "She brought what *I* like."

Suddenly Keely laughed. "What *I* like, you mean!"

For an instant the stiffness between them disappeared. As it settled on them again, Bree looked from one gloomy face to the next. Then she remembered. *It's my job to test Mikkel too.*

When she held out the bread, Bree offered her best smile—the one she used to practice in front of a mirror.

F O U R

THE LONG GOOD-BYE

Mikkel was on his second piece of bread when he bit down on something hard. At first it surprised him. Bree was such a good cook, there shouldn't be anything hard in the food she gave him. Then he saw Bree watching.

Ah ha! Mikkel thought. Bending down, he retied the lace on his leather boot. Quickly he ran his tongue over the hard piece in his mouth. *A small stone?*

Near the large rock where they ate, pebbles lay on the ground. Seeing them, Mikkel felt sure of it. With his tongue he pushed the small stone to the side of his mouth. When he sat up again, he was ready to go on eating.

Now Mikkel caught the gleam in Devin's eyes. *Well, I can play their game, too,* Mikkel decided, even as he wondered why they were testing him. With the stone next to his cheek he chewed carefully, then swallowed.

Suddenly Bree looked concerned. Just as quickly, the look was gone.

When Mikkel took another piece of bread, he found a second stone. This time he pushed it to the other side of his mouth. Bree and Devin still watched.

At first Mikkel thought it was funny. *They wonder what I'll do if they make me angry.* But then Mikkel knew the game was serious. *They want to know if I'll keep my promise. Will I really give Bree her freedom after one voyage?*

For an instant Mikkel promised himself he would do what he had said. After all, his father had given him good reasons for being an honest merchant. But the raid Mikkel led on the Irish monastery had made him a wealthy fourteen-year-old. Now fifteen, he liked thinking about that wealth.

The next moment Mikkel realized the truth. *I don't want to change.* For as long as he could remember he had wanted fame and fortune. Wasn't it good to be ambitious?

"Why don't you give Keely a chance to rest?" Mikkel told Bree. "Talk as long as you want."

When Bree looked up, surprise filled her eyes. "Thanks, Mikkel," she said softly.

As he walked away, he spit the small stones into his

hand. When Bree and Devin weren't looking, he dropped the pebbles to the ground. But he could not leave his thoughts behind.

Instead, he kept thinking about that morning with his parents. "Send her home, Mikkel," his mother had said.

"Look at all Bree and her God have done for us," his father told him. "Look at me." Sigurd stretched out his arms and opened his hands, showing how normal his skin and fingers looked. "I'm clean, clean, clean!"

Grandfather and Grandmother nodded with agreement. "I will miss Bree," Grandmother said. "But do what is right, Mikkel."

Now, like it or not, Mikkel had to look into his own heart. Standing high above the fjord with solid rock beneath his feet, he felt as shaky as if he were looking down into a bottomless pit.

Bree is a valuable slave. The most valuable slave I've ever known.

Then Mikkel knew it was more than that. Like Devin and Keely and the Irish girl, Lil, he didn't want to say good-bye to Bree.

FIVE

WATER MUSIC

As Bree gathered up the last of the food, she again looked down at the farm she had noticed. This time the man she had seen earlier entered the door at one end of the house. Moments later, he came out at the other end of the building.

Am I seeing things? Bree rubbed her eyes.

For almost nine months, she had slept in the hayloft of a barn. She knew exactly how far it was from one end of Sigurd's house to the barn at the other end. Though the house on the mountain below wasn't that big, it was long enough to make Bree curious.

How could that man walk so quickly from one end of the house to the other end of the barn? Did he run the entire way?

When they set out again, Bree and Mikkel went ahead. As they reached an area high on the mountain, he led her over to the rocky edge. Far below, the waters of the fjord seemed bluer than ever before.

From this height Bree could see to the end of the long, narrow waterway. Standing there, she took it in. The great stretch of mountains with snow across the top. The river that flowed through the village of Aurland and emptied into the fjord.

With pride in his voice, Mikkel pointed out the farm where his family had lived for generations. Off in the distance, near the end of the fjord, a waterfall tumbled into the valley below.

For as long as she could remember Bree had been drawn to high places. To her surprise she felt that excitement again, even here in a land that was not her own.

Mikkel's world was different from hers, but Bree had to admit that it was more beautiful than she could have imagined. When she drew a deep breath, Bree found Mikkel watching her.

"Do you like it?" he asked.

"I love it!" To Bree's surprise the beautiful view stripped away the anger she often felt toward Mikkel.

"You know what?" she asked. "Your favorite place is like my favorite place. You look off to the end of a fjord. I look out to the Irish Sea."

But now seeing the long view made Bree lonesome for

the one she had always known. "I've decided something. I want to do my best to make your voyage a success."

"Really?" To Mikkel her words were clearly a happy surprise. "You honestly want to help?"

Bree nodded.

"Why do you want to do that?"

"If I truly help, will you be able to return home faster? Will I get back to Ireland sooner?"

Suddenly the light went out of Mikkel's face. When he spoke, his words were careful. "Maybe. Maybe not. I can't promise. But I could use your help."

"All right. I'll give it."

"Just like that?"

"Just like that." But then Bree saw the hurt in Mikkel's eyes. She had spoiled the gift she truly wanted to offer.

Again Bree looked down the fjord. She wanted to forget that with every opportunity, whether she tried or not, she managed to hurt Mikkel. Would she ever get over her deep-down wish to get even for the way he had changed her life?

Unwilling to ruin her last day with Dev and Keely, Bree pushed her thoughts about Mikkel aside. Her sister needed good memories—something she could hold on to if she ever felt upset about taking Bree's place to go home.

Bree called to her sister. "Come look!"

When Keely joined her, Bree put her arm around her sister's shoulders and pointed to the waterfall farthest down the fjord. "Remember how you loved the streams of Ireland? How you listened after a rain? How you talked about the sound of water running down the sides of our mountains?"

"Water music!" Keely exclaimed.

"When you hear that music again, remember that more than anything else I want you to go back to Ireland—to be with Mam and Daddy again."

As Devin joined them, Bree talked to both of them. "When you're lonesome for me, remember this place. Remember this time we've had together."

HEART OF COURAGE

Suddenly Mikkel could bear it no longer. Quickly he walked away, knowing that if he didn't, he would give in and tell Bree to leave in the morning. And he couldn't do that. He needed Bree so he could succeed— so his journeys would be safe and his trade goods sold. If he couldn't become wealthy by being a raider, he would become a merchant.

I'll be one of the great Vikings, Mikkel promised himself. A man called by that name was held with high honor. He, too, would be a shrewd bargainer and the master of a ship that crossed the stormy seas.

Farther along the overlook, Mikkel stared at the mountains and thought about it. How could he find new markets for trade goods? Become both wealthy and famous? Could he sail to lands he had never seen?

At the edge of the chasm Mikkel stopped, stood there, considered all his choices. *I need to become an explorer. What better way to gain both wealth and fame?*

But last summer when he led the voyage to Ireland, Mikkel had discovered how terrible a storm on the North Sea could be. In the worst of the storm, he had nearly lost heart. What new dangers would he face on a voyage of discovery?

Courage. That's what I need. A heart of courage.

As Mikkel thought about it, he remembered that he still needed a name for his new ship. *Bright courage? Bold of heart? Heart of courage?*

It couldn't be a name that told anyone else what he really wanted. Before his men and his enemies, he could not give that away. Yet he needed a name that reminded him of courage. How could he overcome every difficulty? Go beyond whatever made him afraid?

Suddenly it came to him. "Conquest."

Mikkel spoke the word aloud and liked its sound. "I will conquer all my fears and become rich and famous besides."

Just then Mikkel looked down. Nearby, on a stretch of rocky ground, he saw a coin. As he took a closer look, the sunlight caught the shiny surface.

An Arabic coin, Mikkel thought. *A coin of value.*

It seemed like a good omen. A reminder that his favorite god Thor helped farmers and sailors. The god of physical strength, thunder and lightning, rain and good weather, Thor used his mighty hammer to defend both gods and humans. But now Mikkel could only feel surprise at his good luck.

What was this coin doing on a mountainside? Was it left by some other climber who had been trading in Dublin? Had it slipped out of an open sack of coins?

True, he couldn't use an Arabic coin to buy something here. The present king, Olaf Tryggvason [pronounced *Trigvason*], had been the first in Norway to issue coins. *But if I melt down this coin or take it on my next trip to Ireland—*

As Mikkel looked around for more coins, he glanced toward Bree and Devin. When he wasn't with them, they talked as if they couldn't get their words out fast enough. For a moment Mikkel wished he could be part of that. Then he looked down at the coin.

Once more he glanced in their direction. *It's safe*, he thought.

Scooping up the coin, Mikkel slipped it into a hiding place in his tunic. Already he had plans for it.

SEVEN

DARK SECRET

The next morning Devin stood on the shore near Ingmar's large merchant ship. Men were still rolling barrels and kegs up the ramp onto the ship. But Devin knew that soon his time with Bree would be up.

Dreading that moment, Devin ran his hand through the black hair that had grown shaggy. He wanted nothing to stop his ability to see. And he could not forget one word of what he must say to Bree.

How can I possibly go back to Ireland without this sister I love?

Then Bree stood on the pebbly ground beside him. When she spoke, it was with a strong yet quiet voice that only Devin could hear. "It's not your choice, but mine," she said. "It's my choice that the ransom you intended for me goes to Keely. It's my choice that my friend Lil goes home."

The look in Bree's brown eyes told Devin she would not listen to any argument. Just the same, he tried.

"I can't leave you behind," he said. "I just can't do it."

"You must." Bree's answer came at once. "You had no choice before, and you have no choice now. Keely and Lil need to go home. If you go with Ingmar, he'll keep all of you safe."

For one more moment Devin's gaze held hers. "Mikkel wants me to be his storyteller, and I promised to be his friend. After one voyage, you go free. But we both know that until he deals with the secret he's hiding from his father, Mikkel will always be in trouble."

"Trouble, all right." Bree whispered now. "When Mikkel leaves, what do you think he'll do with the coins he stole?"

Devin shrugged. "I can't begin to guess. But one thing's certain. He can't use them here."

A scared look flitted across Bree's face. "Everyone who came from Ireland on Mikkel's ship knows about the gems he stole from the monastery."

"But not the coins he stole from his father's friend," Devin reminded.

"What if one of those men—"

When Bree shivered, Devin knew it had nothing to

do with the early morning coolness. Mikkel's stolen wealth had already caused enough problems. Was it possible it could cause still more?

Devin spoke quickly now. "Whatever you do, make sure you don't tell Mikkel that you know about Bjorn's coins."

"But what if he makes me so upset that I say too much?"

"If you do, he'll never let you get back to Ireland."

Bree stared at her brother. "If I find a bag of coins, how will I know if they're Bjorn's?"

Glancing around, Devin saw Mikkel headed their way. Without looking down, Devin moved his foot, drawing the side view of a bear in the soft ground.

"Bjorn means bear," he whispered. "It's his stamp in the leather. I saw it on bags at Bjorn's shop."

The instant Bree saw his drawing, Devin shuffled his feet and the design disappeared.

As Keely joined them, Bree opened her arms to hug her younger sister. "The next time I see you, it will be in Ireland."

Bree's voice filled with excitement. "We'll look at each other and say, 'We are *home!*'"

Keely's face shone, as though she knew it to be true. But when she tried to speak, not a word came out. With a grin Bree tugged the long braid that hung over her sister's shoulder. "See you soon."

When her friend Lil drew close, Bree welcomed her with a smile. "No crying."

"I'll miss you." Lil's voice sounded ragged.

"And I'll miss you. For all the ways your voyage to Ireland is difficult and dangerous, remember this: Our God goes before you."

Lil's smile was like a rainbow after a storm. "I'll tell my cousin Tully you're coming home."

Sudden tears welled up in Bree's eyes and spilled over. When she brushed her cheeks, the tears came again. Quickly Bree turned, but in the worst possible direction. Mikkel stood there, watching her. When Bree looked his way, her body stiffened. Instantly she turned back to Lil.

Devin saw the pain in Bree's eyes and moved closer, but Bree spoke to Lil. "Tell Tully—"

Bree stopped. When she started again, her voice still trembled. "Tell Tully I look forward to seeing him when I get home."

Lil stood on tiptoes to kiss Bree's cheek. "Don't ever forget that Tully wants to marry you."

Bree nodded. "I know." Again the tears welled up.

So, Devin told himself, *I always thought it was the three of us who were friends. Me and Tully and Bree. Well, maybe we still are.* But in his mind Devin changed the order of things. *Bree and Tully. Tully and Bree. Someday.*

Devin liked the sound of it, but then he looked toward Mikkel. No doubt about it, he had heard Lil's words. Seeing the thundercloud in Mikkel's eyes, Devin stalked over and stood in front of him. "Be good to my sister," he said.

When Mikkel did not answer, Devin spoke in a voice that Mikkel couldn't ignore. "Take care of Bree," Devin said.

To his surprise, Mikkel stretched out his hand. His anger was gone, and he looked straight into Devin's eyes.

"You have my word for it. My promise."

For a moment Devin waited, hand at his side. Standing there, he searched Mikkel's face. "I can trust you?" Devin asked.

"You can trust me," Mikkel said. "And you'll come back?"

"I'm planning on it."

As though suddenly remembering, Mikkel shoved a hand into his tunic and drew out a coin. Still watching Devin's face, Mikkel handed it to him.

"It's not mine," Mikkel said. "Is it yours?"

Devin nodded, but swallowed hard. He had found it difficult to drop his last coin from Bjorn high on the mountain. *So Mikkel passed every test Bree and I tried. But how long will his big heart last?*

Much as he wanted to hope, Devin found it hard to believe that Mikkel could really make a change. When he offered his hand again, Devin shook it, and then closed his other hand over Mikkel's. "When I return, I'll meet your ship at the settlement surrounded by seven mountains."

Without another word Mikkel walked quickly away. A short distance up the slope he stopped as though holding himself apart from all the good-byes.

For one moment longer Devin studied Bree's face, memorizing the way she looked. Daddy and Mam, Adam, Cara, and Jen would ask him for every detail. But there was something more. Neither Devin nor Bree could be sure they would ever see each other again.

"Remember," she said. "I've told you to not come back. It's too dangerous."

"But you still need to get home," Devin said quietly.

"I'll find a way. If Daddy and Mam tell you not to come, you have to obey."

Devin knew that was true, but he could only cry out in his heart, *They must not tell me I can't come back!*

As though understanding how hard that would be, Bree watched him with the solemn look of a schoolteacher. Then her old laugh welled up and bubbled over. At the good Irish sound, Devin grinned back.

Ingmar was ready now, his ship loaded and men waiting. As Ingmar called to Devin, Bree bent down to pick up a small rock from the shore. "Courage to win, Dev," she said as she handed it to him. When Bree smiled, her eyes were again wet with tears.

For Devin, seeing Bree smile was the worst of all.

"Courage to win, Bree," he said, giving her a quick brotherly hug.

Turning away at once, he picked up his bundles of food and clothing. Without another look back, Devin led Keely and Lil to the ship.

They had barely stepped onto the proud merchant ship when men pulled up the ramp. As other Vikings lifted the stone anchor, Devin took Keely and Lil to the stern. Standing there, they looked back as the oars dipped and the ship moved away. But Devin watched only one person.

Bree stood straight and strong on the shore next to the deep blue water. As the distance between her and the ship widened, she grew smaller. Suddenly she lifted her right arm and pointed to the sky.

Moments later, the ship rounded the bend in the fjord, and Devin saw Bree no more.

EIGHT

BREE'S NEW PLAN

As soon as Ingmar's ship passed from sight, Bree turned away. Without a word she headed for the straight-up-and-down mountain at one side of the farm. Walking as fast as she could, Bree took the narrow path to her favorite hollow between the rocks. Only when she was out of sight of everyone did she allow her tears to come.

When at last Bree stopped weeping, she hated herself. *The big older sister who helps everyone else,* she thought, as she remembered her good-byes to Keely and Lil. Even with Dev she had almost changed places in their brother-sister relationship. Though he had always taken care of her, she had done her best to show him that she would be all right. But now Bree felt only despair.

Wherever she looked, Bree saw only three faces—Dev, Keely, and Lil. With every thought she said good-bye again. With every stab of hurt, she wondered if she had done the right thing, giving up her opportunity to return to Ireland. *But what other choice did I have?*

Keely and Lil needed to go home. Already Bree felt a loneliness that tore her apart. No one, especially Mikkel, would know how much she hurt inside. But Bree knew her own weaknesses. Too often she spit out exactly what she thought.

Soon Mikkel and his new crew would travel long distances together. Up the coast of Norway to Nidaros where the king lived. Then all the way to Iceland and back. Through perils of the open sea and dangers that would come even when people worked together. Through accidents that might happen because people didn't like one another.

Thinking about the possibilities, Bree felt cold with dread. Then as tears blurred her sight, she remembered words she had memorized long ago. *Do not be afraid, for I have ransomed you—*

Bree sat there, stunned. *I gave the ransom for two others to go home. But Jesus ransomed me! Paid the price and set me free!*

Filled with the wonder of a promise she desperately needed, Bree looked out on the fjord. The beauty of the water and sky surrounded her. And the quiet voice she knew went on.

I have called you by name—

Soon after her capture by Vikings, Bree had sensed God speaking to her heart, calling her to be a light to the nations. Since then Bree had often wondered what that call from God meant.

Now, as clearly as if someone had spoken aloud, she heard the rest of His promise. *I have called you by name; you are mine.*

Bowing her head, Bree rested her face on a large rock and started to pray.

When you go through deep waters and great trouble, I will be with you. When you go through rivers of difficulty, you will not drown!

As Bree took a deep breath, she felt His peace. *For I am the Lord, your God, the Holy One of Israel.*

When she stood up, Bree knew what to do. Going down to the fjord, she splashed cold water on her face. Pinching her cheeks, she tried to hide her tears. As she started back to the farm, she walked tall. Though she looked like a warrior going to battle, a smile lit her face.

In all the months of working for Mikkel as a silver-smith, she had not found one clue to lead her to Mikkel's treasure. But Dev had told her to keep looking for Bjorn's coins. She would begin.

Soon Bree drew close to the long shed next to the fjord. There Mikkel had built his new longship. Now she heard him whistling.

Whistling.

Just hearing him made Bree angry.

Whistling when I cried for what seemed forever? Doesn't Mikkel care what just happened to me?

For a moment Bree stood outside the shed, wanting only to find a way to get even. But then she remembered the words that comforted her. *I have called you by name; you are mine.*

Bree sighed. Sometimes it wasn't much fun being called by name. *All right, God,* Bree told Him. *I'll do my best to be civil to Mikkel. Not friendly. Barely polite. Civil.*

When she stepped into the boat shed, Bree saw Mikkel's nearly completed ship still on supports. Chips of wood lay on the ground and shelves held the tools of his trade.

Mikkel sat on a high stool next to his worktable. Long, narrow strips of wood called staves lay in front of him. When put together, they interlocked, making a watertight barrel, keg, or tub.

When Mikkel saw Bree, he looked startled. After one swift movement of his hand, he grinned, but Bree wasn't fooled.

He's hiding something, she decided. Pretending she hadn't noticed, she walked closer. As though it wasn't important, Mikkel set more staves on top of whatever he had covered. But Bree acted curious about an oar on the worktable.

The pole was long and sturdy and the blade for rowing carefully shaped. On the end where an oarsman grasped the pole, it had a round bulge. Running her hand over the bulge, Bree asked, "What's this?"

As though glad she was interested in that instead of whatever he had hidden, Mikkel took the oar over to his ship. Close to the rails were several holes with horizontal slits on each side. Reaching into the ship, Mikkel slipped the blade of the oar through a hole. The slits made it possible for the blade to pass through, but the bulge in the pole kept the oar from going too far.

Bree caught the reason at once. "So you don't lose an oar in the water."

Mikkel grinned. "Don't we Vikings know how to make ships?"

Pride filled his voice. When he turned back to his workbench, pride still lit his face.

Sitting down on his stool, he picked up his ax and started working on a stave that was nearly finished. But now Bree noticed the dragonhead for the front of Mikkel's ship. The fierce-looking head upset her.

As though only a day had passed, Bree remembered sailing away from Ireland with a dragonhead towering above her. The setting sun had cast a red light on the large head. Like a giant serpent, it rose up with snarling mouth, dark and fearful.

"When I came here on your ship I was afraid of your dragon," Bree said.

"Good." Mikkel grinned. "That's what I want. A dragon should look so fierce that it frightens away evil spirits."

Bree glared at him. "If you think that stupid head will protect you, you're wrong!"

Suddenly Mikkel's ax slipped, making a gash in the wood on which he worked. "Now see what you did!"

"I didn't do it! You can't blame me."

"You come in here and talk. You keep asking questions!"

But Bree felt angry. Even more, she felt upset about what Mikkel believed. Would he ever understand that God wanted to help him?

Then Bree remembered the strange sense that she was supposed to come in here for some reason. What was Mikkel really hiding?

"I'm sorry," she said, then felt surprised at her apology. "Can you still use the stave?"

Mikkel shrugged, obviously wanting her to leave. As she started for the door, Bree thought of the voyage ahead. If they were once again enemies, it would be harder every step of the way.

Turning back, she said, "Mikkel, I meant what I said on the mountain. I really want to help. I'll work hard to make your voyage a success."

"I know. So you can go home quicker." Mikkel did not look up.

Before Ingmar left, the fishermen-farmers had planted their crops and taken their animals across the fjord. The cows and their calves, as well as the goats, munched plentiful grass at the bottom of the mountain. Soon they would be taken up to the summer pasture.

Some time before, men had cut down trees, stripped them of bark, and allowed them to dry. Now they carried the logs down to the shore. Each day fishermen hung their catch on drying racks, and women and girls baked flatbread for the coming voyage. Bree and Rika finished the huge sail for Mikkel's new ship.

Thread by thread, line by line, they had woven pieces of that sail, and then sewn the sections together. When Bree took the last stitch, she ran her hand across the cloth on which they had worked all winter. Made with the unwashed wool of longhaired sheep, the lanolin in the yarn helped to waterproof the sail.

Before turning it over to Mikkel, Rika carefully checked each seam. She wanted no stitch to loosen, allowing weakness in the sail when the great winds filled it.

On the day the ship was to be launched, it seemed that everyone from the entire area gathered near the long shed next to the fjord. A number of men climbed into the ship and stood at the stern. When the prow lifted off the ground, other men set four- to five-foot lengths of tree trunks in place. Stripped of bark, the logs lay parallel to each other and about three feet apart.

When the front of the ship dropped down, the pieces of wood became a runway. Men at the stern pushed at the hull, and the ship slid into the water. For an instant the hull bobbled, then settled fair and true.

Mikkel's face shone like the sun breaking through clouds. Arms high in the air, he shouted his excitement. Splashing through the water, Mikkel reached the ship, grabbed hold of the side, and swung aboard.

Working together, he and other men set the mast in place. When his men brought the huge sail from the long-house, Mikkel's mother Rika stood on the shore next to them. Already she had lost one son to the sea, but no trace of that sorrow showed on her face. Instead, Rika made a proud ceremony of giving the new sail to Mikkel.

Respectfully bowing to his mother, Mikkel took it with a smile and a thank-you. At first Mikkel ran the sail up slowly as if to show its splendor. Then with a quick snap he brought it the rest of the way.

Standing back, Mikkel looked up. As a light breeze filled the sail, it billowed out, a thing of beauty.

At first Mikkel stared at it, as though not believing the ship was really his. Then he walked over to the mast and ran his hand along the tall, strong pole. When he turned to the people on shore, his excitement shone in his face.

"What will you call her?" asked a man in the crowd.

Mikkel grinned. "Our king named one of his ships the *Short Serpent*. And now his mighty *Long Serpent* is the largest ship in our land."

Mikkel rested his hand on the smooth surface of the rail. "I name this ship *Conquest*, for we will know the victory of the seas!"

A nearby crewmember grinned his agreement. As Mikkel raised his arms again, a shout went up.

"*Conquest!*" A man on the shore called out the name, and the crowd echoed it back.

"*Conquest!*" Mikkel shouted again. "To succeed. Overcome. Conquer. You'll see!"

But Bree turned away, not wanting anyone to see her face. Would this ship that made Mikkel so proud be used for battle? Or even worse, for raids on innocent people? Or would it truly help him overcome the dangers he would face on every side? The loneliness was back in Bree's heart, and she didn't want anyone to know.

With Mikkel's ship launched, men began loading the *Conquest* and Sigurd's ship, the *Sea Bird*. Logs were stored on both sides of the mast, lashed together, and tied down. Mikkel watched everything that came on board to be sure the load was balanced.

When the dried fish was ready to take off the lines, Rika showed Bree how to pack it in wooden kegs. Already the dry, crisp flatbread was stored in airtight chests.

The next morning Rika gave Bree a new sea chest of her own. Rika's kindness surprised Bree. She had come to Aurland with only the clothes on her back and the bag of supplies her Irish friend Nola had given her.

That afternoon, men started coming in from farms far and near, mountains, and valleys. In the crowd of people around the ships, Bree noticed a man who seemed familiar. Like others, he carried a sea chest he set down in the front of the ship.

Of average height, the man had hands like hammers, broad shoulders, and muscular arms. Bree knew he was used to hard work. Though he looked strong, he moved as quickly and silently as a cat.

For a moment Bree stared at him. Why did she feel as if she knew him?

Around Bree, the men were so busy that she wanted only to get out of their way. When she started down the wooden ramp between ship and shore, she saw the same man with broad shoulders. How had he managed to reach shore before she did?

Then Bree forgot her question. Right in front of her stood her Irish friend, Nola. Bree hadn't seen her since their arrival in Aurland.

"You're coming with?" Bree asked, throwing her arms around her.

One of the captives taken by Vikings, Nola had helped Bree in every way she could. With the same black hair and blue eyes as Devin, Nola had always been lovely in the way she cared about others. But now there was a softness to her. "I'm married," she explained.

Bree felt glad for her. "To one of the Irish?"

Nola smiled. "One of the Norwegians."

"You married a Norseman?" Bree couldn't think of anything worse. "Are you serious? How could a good Irish woman like you ever marry a man from the North?"

The moment the words spilled from her lips, Bree clapped her hands over her mouth. "Oh, I'm sorry."

But Nola laughed. Reaching out, she tugged the arm of one of the men. "This is my husband, Garth."

When Nola pulled him over, Bree looked into the face of the man she had just noticed. Now he carried two sea chests, one on each shoulder.

Suddenly Bree knew why he seemed familiar. "You live high on the mountain," she said.

"Garth decided I would make a better wife than a slave," Nola explained. For an instant she laid her hand on his muscular arm. When he flushed with embarrassment, she let go. Just the same, Bree noticed the light in Garth's eyes when he looked at Nola.

That evening those who lived farther away slept in one of the ships or in tents on shore. Bree worked far into the night to finish packing the dried fish. By the time she set the last cover in place, it was very dark. Picking up the keg, she started toward Mikkel's ship.

As she walked down to the shore she saw that the number of tents had grown. The area was quiet for the first time in days. Making no sound, Bree hurried onto the *Conquest* and looked for an open spot near the stern. When she found it, she set the keg down.

As she started to leave, Bree noticed a shadow darker than the night. When it moved, Bree froze. There was no mistaking it. Someone searched among the kegs and barrels at the front of the longship. Who was creeping around the ship while everyone else slept?

Without thinking, Bree started in that direction. Suddenly she felt a warning. What could be more dangerous than scaring someone who shouldn't be there?

Her heart thumping, Bree dropped to her knees. Hiding behind barrels, she listened. When all was quiet, she started crawling on her hands and knees. She had nearly reached the ramp off the ship when she heard a quiet bump. The sound of a keg or barrel being moved.

A secret sound, thought Bree. *Someone trying to not be seen. What is going on?*

NINE

DUBLIN

When Ingmar's proud merchant ship reached the Norwegian Sea, the winds blew fair. Even across the North Sea, which was known for its storms, the ship made steady progress toward the southwest. As they sailed through the Hebrides, Devin watched for markers along the way.

With each day that passed he grew more excited. Deep in his heart Devin always felt an ache about leaving Bree. But when the wind filled the great square sail, Devin looked at Keely and Lil and thought about bringing them home.

Whether Devin worked along with the Norsemen or stood at the side of the ship, he watched for anything he recognized. A week after leaving the Aurland Fjord, he and Keely and Lil caught their first glimpse of the white cliffs of Rathlin Island.

Soon Devin spotted the high bluff named Fair Head. From there the ship sailed down the east coast of Ireland. As the Mountains of Mourne swept down to the sea, Devin told the girls how he drank water from the hollow of six-sided stones that stood like pillars on the north coast.

One morning as Ingmar sailed closer to land, he came to stand at the rail with Devin. During their first voyage together, Devin had learned to value the strength and courage of this young man only four or five years older than he. With blue eyes and a face bronzed by the sun, Ingmar spoke in a voice quiet enough for Devin's ears alone.

"What will you do about Bree?" he asked.

"Go back to her." The words left Devin's mouth like an arrow from its bow. He thought of little else.

"You understand how dangerous it is? They may take you again."

"I know." Devin held no doubt about the danger involved.

"Then why do you think of going back? What if I'm not there to help you?"

"I'll go back because I must. Bree is my sister."

"But who do you trust?"

"Mikkel's father Sigurd. Mikkel's mother Rika."

Ingmar nodded. "Yes. They are worthy of trust. But Mikkel? Are you forgetting Mikkel?"

"No," answered Devin. "I can never forget Mikkel."

As he spoke, a deeply felt anger welled up within Devin. Then he remembered Bree's constant struggle to forgive. Difficult as it was for him, Devin knew he again needed to put his anger aside.

"Mikkel promised that if Bree and I went with him for one voyage, he would set her free."

Surprise filled Ingmar's eyes. "And you believe him? If Mikkel treats you badly, he'll hide it from his father. You don't trust Mikkel, do you?"

Devin grinned. "Only with my eyes open. And both eyes on Mikkel."

Ingmar sighed. "I don't like it. I wish you wouldn't go back. But then there's Bree."

Devin felt the pain of it again. "Always there's Bree."

"Yes." Ingmar looked out across the sea. "She's the kind of girl a young man wants to marry."

Startled, Devin tried to see Ingmar's eyes, but his face was turned away. As Bree's brother, Devin had never thought about how a young man such as Ingmar might see her. Usually Devin didn't even notice that she was becoming a beautiful young woman. Not until Lil talked about Tully had Devin thought about the possibility that one day his sister would marry.

Tully and Bree. Devin tried the sound of it again. *If Bree married Tully, it would be good.*

But not yet, Devin told himself. *Bree is years away from marrying.*

His face thoughtful, Ingmar still looked off to sea. *Bree and Ingmar.* The thought came before Devin could push it aside. *Ingmar and Bree. No!*

Much as Devin respected the kind master of the merchant ship, much as Devin appreciated his protection—

Bree must marry an Irishman. No one else, no matter how good the man is. Bree must come home, live near our family for the rest of her life.

Ingmar turned, facing Devin again. "I don't like it. Your going back, I mean. But if you decide to return for Bree, come to my ship fourteen days from now. Don't be late, or I'll have to sail without you."

As the tides of the Irish Sea met the waters of the River Liffey, Ingmar asked a question. "Devin, there's a courage about you I don't understand. Who do you really trust?"

Ahhhh. Just thinking about Ingmar's question, Devin felt better. As this Norseman, this man of the North, sailed into Ireland, Devin explained. When he finished, Ingmar asked, "And Bree? Does she believe the same way?"

Again Devin felt the pain of Ingmar's interest in Bree. But when Devin spoke, his voice was steady. "Bree believes the same way. Our whole family believes in the Christian God, Jesus."

Farther upriver, the ship came to the high earth embankment that formed a circle around the city of Dublin. Named *Dubhlinn* or "black pool" from the dark color of the River Liffey, it was the first true town in Ireland. The water was indeed dark, but now in the early morning light it reflected the buildings along the river.

Dublin was an independent Norse kingdom—a trade center established by Vikings from the North Atlantic. Devin's father came here to trade, and Bree and Devin had learned the Norse language from him.

On top of the high embankment around Dublin a tall fence of upright timbers gave added protection. As Ingmar's ship drew close to the shore, his men took up oars and guided it in. Others leaped over the side of the ship and made it secure.

Devin led the way off the ship. When Keely stepped down on Irish ground, she dropped to her knees and kissed the soil. When Lil did the same thing, Devin felt embarrassed.

Glancing around, he hoped that the ship's crew was too busy to notice. But Ingmar had stopped working to watch.

"A thousand thank-yous," Devin called out. "Thank you more than I can say for bringing us home."

But Ingmar understood. "When Bree returns to Ireland, she, too, will kiss the land. When I reach home I stay on my feet, but I like to stand on my own soil."

When Keely and Lil said good-bye to Ingmar he accepted their thanks, but warned Devin again. "Be sure you're here in fourteen days. Not a moment later, or you'll miss my ship."

"I'll be back," Devin said with all the certainty he could manage. "I need to meet Mikkel and keep my promise."

"If you're not here, I'll know that you and your family decided you shouldn't go."

A tight band of grief tightened Devin's chest, welled up in his throat. "I have to go back," he said. "For Bree's sake, I must go back."

Ingmar's solemn eyes met his. "Farewell, my friend. I will learn to pray to your God. To ask Him to keep you and Bree safe."

With a bundle on his back and two more bundles beneath an arm, Devin led the way for Keely and Lil. Wide timbers, cut flat and square, lay along the shore near the ship. Set close together, they formed a wooden path across ground made soft by the incoming tide.

To Devin's surprise he remembered the way as though he had left Dublin only yesterday. As the ground rose steeply, steps led to an opening in the wall surrounding the city. Devin took the wide path before him, then turned onto a narrower street.

Fishermen just in from their morning catch called out, "Fish for sale! Fish for sale!" Up and down the streets they walked, making their way between rumbling carts and squawking chickens. As before, Devin felt overwhelmed by the noise and people and longed to be home.

But first he must find his Norwegian friend Bjorn. Through one street after another Devin passed houses with thatched roofs that looked strangely Irish, though built by Norsemen. And then he was there, standing in the doorway of the cobbler's shop.

"Devin!" Bjorn exclaimed the moment he saw him. "Come in, my friend." Setting down his cobbler's hammer, he stepped around the workbench where he was making shoes. "You are back! And all is well?"

Devin grinned. "Almost well."

Bjorn looked beyond him. Keely stood behind Devin. "This is Bree?"

Devin shook his head. "This is Keely, my younger sister who was stolen away by Vikings seven summers ago."

"Really!" Bjorn met her gaze. "Welcome home, Keely," Bjorn said softly. "Welcome to Dublin—to good Irish sod, even though we Norsemen walk upon it."

When Keely's shy smile spread across her face, Bjorn went on. "Soon you will be truly home. You will open the door of your cottage and your Mamma and Pappa will put their arms around you."

Keely's eyes glowed, as though the thought of it warmed the tucked-away spots in her heart.

Bjorn turned to Lil. "And this is Bree?" he asked again.

"I'm Lil," she said at once. "I'm a Byrne from the Wicklow Mountains."

"And proud of it, you are!"

"And right proud of Bree. She took care of me, and then she made a necklace—"

"The hacksilver?" Bjorn asked Devin. Viking raiders shared loot among themselves by hacking up their plunder. Often used for barter, the silver pieces were cut from larger pieces such as silver vessels or jewelry. Pieces of hacksilver were weighed to give a common exchange.

"*Your* hacksilver," Devin answered. "The small bits and pieces you gave me, the large beautiful chunk, and the silver loop of wire. Yes, Bree made a necklace."

"So!" In his delight Bjorn slapped his hand on his worktable. "One Norseman paying another Norseman the ransom to set this child free?" Bjorn grinned at Lil, then at Devin. "It is good. It is the way peace is built."

But when Bjorn looked back at Devin, his eyes were serious again. "And Bree? You still don't have her?"

When Devin's throat tightened he shook his head, unable to speak.

Bjorn stretched out his big hand, clapped Devin on the shoulder. "What happened, my friend?"

Swallowing hard, Devin tried to push down the lump in his throat.

"The ransom you brought?" Bjorn asked.

When Devin could speak, he explained all that had

happened. Then he added, "I'll bring Keely and Lil home. We'll celebrate and hear the glad cries of the Irish. And then I'll go back to get Bree."

"No!" Bjorn's voice was as sudden and startling as a clap of thunder.

"No?" Devin asked. "But I must. I can't leave Bree there."

"She must find another way home," Bjorn warned.

"No!" Devin cried. The pain within him spilled out into the cobbler's shop. "I promised I would go back."

"And who did you promise?" Bjorn asked.

"I told Mikkel I would be his storyteller and I would be his friend. He promised that if Bree and I went with him on one voyage, he would set her free when he reached home again."

"Mikkel!" Bjorn spat upon the earthen floor. "That's how much a promise from Mikkel is worth!"

Bjorn turned to the two girls. "Please. Wait outside."

When Keely and Lil shut the door behind them, Bjorn spoke again. "The bag of silver coins Mikkel stole from me. Did you learn anything about the coins?"

Devin's shoulders slumped. "Nothing. Bree and an Irishman worked as silversmiths. But neither of them could figure out where Mikkel hid his treasure. Each morning he gave them only enough silver for the work of that day."

"Mikkel." Slowly Bjorn sat down on the high stool he

used while making shoes. Leaning forward, he set his elbows on the table, then his chin upon his hands. "And you truly believe Mikkel will keep his promise? That at the end of one voyage he will allow both you and Bree to return home?"

For what seemed forever, Devin looked down at his feet. He was still wearing the leather boots Bjorn had made him. *Mikkel.*

Devin sighed. *Always Mikkel.*

Looking up, Devin spoke in a quiet voice. "I *want* to believe that Mikkel will keep his promise."

"You *want!*" When Bjorn pounded his fist on the table, it rattled. "You *want* to believe! It is not enough. You cannot trust Mikkel. If someone would steal from his father's best friend—"

"I know." Devin's voice was so small that he felt as if he had not spoken. "And I didn't find the coins for you, as I hoped. I'll try again when I go back."

But Bjorn held up his hands. "No! Don't ever go back for the coins. It's not worth it to me, nor to anyone else."

Standing up, Bjorn leaned close to be sure that Devin understood. "Talk to your Mamma and Pappa. Listen to them. You and your parents must decide whether you should go back for Bree. But don't ever go back for the coins."

"Not return for Bree?" To Devin it was unthinkable. Yet two Norsemen, two men from the North, had warned him not to go back.

Devin's long sigh seemed to fill the room. "And now I must go home and tell my parents I don't have Bree. Yes, I have Keely and Lil. But Bree is still not with us."

Like a kind, giant bear, Bjorn spoke in a voice filled with caring. "You want to trust Mikkel because it gives you hope."

Devin nodded. "It gives me hope."

"But can you *really* trust him?"

"I don't know." Devin looked up into the face of his kind Norwegian friend. "I always wondered if Mikkel's greed would win out." Mikkel's return of the coin still puzzled Devin.

"Mikkel is filled with greed, and he wants to be famous," Devin said quietly. "I can't guess what that might cause him to do, but—"

"But what?"

"I want to believe that Mikkel can change."

TEN

THE BIG MYSTERY

Early the next morning, Bree stood at the stern of Mikkel's ship and looked back. As they sailed from Aurland, his mother Rika stood on the shore, along with Cort and the grandparents. To Bree's surprise she felt a tinge of sadness that she quickly pushed away.

Silly as a goose, she told herself. Just the same, she wondered if she would ever see Mikkel's family again.

As they rounded the bend in the fjord, Bree still looked back. Then the high rock walls on either side of the narrow waterway hid the village of Aurland. When Bree faced forward, she felt as if she was beginning a new life.

On her trip here she had often been afraid. Countless

times she had wondered, *What will it be like being a slave?*
By now Bree had changed in as many ways as she had once
been afraid.

Just the same, she knelt down to where the dog
Shadow lay at her feet. As she stroked his back, Bree felt
glad that he had followed her on board. She still felt surprised that Mikkel let the dog stay.

Sailing ahead of them, Sigurd's ship, the *Sea Bird,* led
them on. Whenever Bree glanced at Mikkel, she saw the
excitement in his face. It wasn't hard to tell how much he
liked his new ship and the way she handled. By the time
both ships reached the broad waters of the Sognefjord
[*Songnefyord*], Bree knew something else. Now that she
didn't feel so frightened and alone, she liked to sail.

Their first night out, the two ships stopped in a sheltered bay. As Bree watched, the muscular man she remembered as Nola's husband carried the heavy cooking pots
from the *Conquest.* But when Nola asked for the tripod to
be set in a certain place Garth ignored her.

Nola poked his arm and pointed. "Over there. Out
of the wind."

But the man shook his head. Setting the tripod in a
different place, he spread the three legs wide and hung an
iron pot from the chain.

The moment he went back to the ship, Nola un-
hooked the pot, lifted the tripod, and set it down where
she wanted it. By the time Garth returned, she had filled

the pot with water and laid the fire. Garth took one look
at her, turned, and walked off. Nola ignored him.

As Bree filled another pot with water she wondered
about it. Nola thought it was good, being married to this
man? As far as Bree was concerned, her friend was still
being treated like a slave.

The next morning fog lay heavy upon the water. Out
of long habit, Bree prepared the porridge without thinking. But when she served it, she jerked wide awake.
Directly in front of her stood two men that looked so
identical that Bree forgot to serve them.

"You're twins?" she asked. When both of them grinned,
Bree could only stare. How could their smile be just the
same?

"I'm Garth," said one.

"I'm Hammer," said the other.

Even seeing them together, Bree couldn't tell which
one was Nola's husband. Then Bree remembered to keep
the line moving.

"Garth has a twin?" she asked Nola later. "I can't tell
them apart."

"Most people can't. But I've never missed once."

Bree looked at Nola, then back at the men. "How do
you know?"

"Not by the way they work. Not by their clothes.
When one doesn't know what the other is wearing they
still manage to put on the same thing. Garth hates it. He

tells his brother to go back and change. But Hammer likes it."

"How can I tell them apart?"

"Just wait," Nola told her. "You'll know."

Bree doubted it. Every time she looked at the twins, she saw more ways in which they were alike. As with many of the men on board, they had strong shoulders and muscular arms from the work they did. Yet both of the twins also had fists as powerful as a hammer. And both seemed to move as quickly and silently as a cat.

Watching them, something bothered Bree. She still felt as if she knew the men before seeing them at the farm. Yet she also felt certain that she would have remembered twins. With all her heart, Bree hoped she would never need to recognize which one was which.

That day the ships left the Sognefjord behind and turned north along the jagged coast of the Norwegian Sea. Much as Bree had wanted to know what lay beyond the Irish Sea, nothing had prepared her for this.

By now she knew that a warm current flowed along the coast. At times they passed between skerries, the small rocky islands that formed a barrier against the waves of the sea. Often the land gave way to bays and fjords—long arms of water reaching inward between straight-up-and-down mountains. As they sailed up the west coast, Bree heard the men call it *norveg*, the way to the North.

Bree tried to take in everything. Sometimes she simply looked up to the blue sky and watched as seagulls fluttered down to settle on the water. Other times she stood at the rail, feeling the spray of saltwater against her face. Deep inside, Bree felt sure of one thing. No one could steal away the peace she felt—not unless she let them.

When they finished eating their evening meal, Sigurd, Mikkel, and their men sat around the fire, playing chess or telling stories. One evening they started talking about King Olaf Tryggvason.

"Not long ago he was a Viking raider," said Nola's husband. At least Bree thought it was Garth. If one of the twins talked very much, it seemed to be him.

"When Olaf became a Christian, he stopped his raids on England," Garth went on.

"What is the king like?" Bree asked, as curious as always.

"King Olaf is bolder and taller, more handsome than all other men," Garth told her. "He's the greatest in all kinds of sports. Strong and limber, a good climber. One of his guardsmen climbed to the top of a high mountain and couldn't get down. King Olaf went after the man and carried him down."

"He *carried* him?" Bree couldn't imagine the strength it would take to carry a man down a steep mountainside.

"Is it true that the king juggles swords?" Mikkel asked.

Garth grinned. "Three at a time. One is always up in

the air. Another he grabs by the hilt. And the third flies somewhere between."

"He uses his sword just as well with either hand," said another man. "He can throw two spears at one time. But best of all—"

Mikkel leaned forward. "Best of all, he runs on the oars outside his ship when the men are rowing."

"Are you serious?" Bree asked.

Mikkel grinned. "I've heard it from at least ten men. I've always wanted to try it."

In her mind Bree could see it. A very tall man, blond, no doubt, leaping along the oars not far above the water. And if the oars were going up and down—if he missed even one of them—

Bree laughed. Around the fire many of the men joined her. But then the talk turned to more serious things. When Garth began talking about the new religion, Nola stopped washing the cooking pots and listened. Bree felt sure that Nola cared deeply about what her husband believed.

"Since becoming king, Olaf Tryggvason has gone from one area to another, talking to people about becoming Christians. When he asked the landowners of Rogaland to gather for an assembly, the men were angry."

Rogaland was an area along the southwestern coast. Bree had heard about one of its high, sheer drops into the water below.

"When all the men gathered, they were fully

weaponed," Garth went on. "They chose three men— landowners who were the best speakers—to answer the king and speak against him. When King Olaf came, he told them he wished them to take up Christianity. When the king ended his speech, the landowner who spoke best stood up to answer."

"And King Olaf? What did he do?" Mikkel asked.

"When the landowner tried to speak, there came upon him such a cough and choking that he couldn't bring forth a word. He sat down."

Around the fire the men laughed.

"With all courage the second landowner stood up," Garth said. "He would not be discouraged, in spite of what happened to the other man. But when the second man began to speak, he stammered so much that he couldn't bring forth a single word. When everyone started to laugh, the landowner sat down."

Here and there Bree saw a grin, but no one spoke. Garth paused, looked from one man to the next.

"So the third man stood up. He also planned to speak against King Olaf and his beliefs. But his voice was so hoarse and his speech so thick that no one could hear what he said. He, too, had to sit down."

This time no one around the campfire laughed. Instead, one man looked at another, then glanced away. Silent now, every man seemed to be thinking. Here and there Bree saw a look of dread. If the king tried to change their old beliefs in Odin and Thor, what would they do?

It was Mikkel who asked, "And then?"

"There was no one else to try to speak against the king. Instead, everyone agreed to do what he asked. All the people at the assembly were baptized before the king left."

Bree smiled, glad that the meeting with King Olaf ended so well. But then she looked toward Nola. Her friend stood near the fire, waiting, as if wondering whether her husband would say more.

Watching Nola, Bree knew that something was wrong. *Why did Garth stop? What isn't he saying?*

When Garth didn't speak again, Bree glanced toward Mikkel. The scowl on his face went deep. But it was Sigurd who interested Bree most. No doubt about it, he looked troubled.

Why? Bree wondered. *What do Garth and Sigurd and Mikkel know that I don't know? Why is it so important?*

Later, as the men separated, heading for their tents, Bree heard the low voice of one man talking to another. "If you're the king's friend, it's all right," he said, his voice dark with dread. "But it's not good to be his enemy."

❁

As they headed north the next morning, men fished from both ships. In late afternoon Sigurd stopped at a small cove, but Mikkel sailed on. When the clouds above them darkened, waves dashed against the rocks.

No longer did a chain of small islands give them protection. Instead, whitecaps edged the waves. Deep swells pounded against the shore, washing over all that lay before them. Around a turn in the land, the *Conquest* slipped into calmer waters. The moment they brought the ship up onshore, each man hurried to his duties.

Moving quickly, they unloaded the large iron kettles in which Bree and Nola made soup. Others finished cleaning the fish caught on the way. Still others headed for a clear stream of water that tumbled down the mountain into the sea.

Bree had no doubt that the men wanted food before the rains came. When she and Nola returned from gathering driftwood, they found the large cooking pots hanging from their three-legged stands. As soon as the water started to boil, Bree dropped the cleaned fish into the pots.

Heavy black clouds had drawn close by the time Bree started to dish up food. With an eye on the sky, the men filed through quickly, sat down, and began eating. Suddenly Mikkel spit out his food.

"What did you do with this?" he asked Bree.

"Do? The same thing I do every time I make fish soup."

Next to Mikkel a man gagged. Another coughed. A

third held his throat as if the back of his mouth burned. Still another stood up, walked away, and threw his food to the birds.

"This is your good cook?" he asked Mikkel. "Stop bragging about her!"

"So!" Mikkel's angry words spilled out at Bree. "You said you were going to help me."

"I am." Bree felt both embarrassed and angry. But Mikkel kept on. "Is this what you call help?"

Jumping up, he tossed out the rest of his soup and walked over to the second kettle. Nola still stood there, dishing up. "Please," Mikkel told her respectfully.

Nola filled it to the brim. As Mikkel passed Bree he glared at her. "Promised to help! Sure! Stones in the bread first. Now this."

Bree was embarrassed. Until now, Mikkel hadn't mentioned the stones. Did he have to do it before all his men?

Sitting down again, Mikkel dug his spoon into the soup and filled his mouth. A moment later, he spit everything out.

This time Mikkel's anger took in Nola. "All right, tell us. What are the two of you up to?"

But his men were not waiting for an answer. Each one emptied his bowl on the ground and headed for the third kettle. This time Nola dished up only half a bowl. "What's wrong?" she asked as they came through the line.

"It's terrible," one said. "Makes me gag."

"Parches my mouth," said another.

Suddenly Mikkel stopped the men at the third kettle. "Don't eat any more of it," he said. "This soup is made with salt water instead of fresh."

As Mikkel looked around, his eyes were as blue as the sea. His flyaway blond hair stood out in the wind. An angry flush darkened his sunburned face.

"The day's catch is ruined," he said. "Who did it?"

When no one spoke up, Mikkel tried again. "Tell me. Who collected the water?"

Three men stepped forward. Bree watched them. One was a man she believed to be Nola's husband, Garth. Another was one of Mikkel's trusted relatives from Aurland. The third was unknown to Bree, but someone she had seen working with Mikkel before. Why would such men get water from the ocean instead of a stream? It didn't make sense.

Then a sudden gust of wind whipped along the coast. With a great clap of thunder the heavens opened, and everyone ran for shelter.

On the way, Bree tripped over a wooden bucket. Suddenly she stopped. *Now what is that bucket doing here?*

As rain poured down upon her, Bree started back to where three cooking pots still hung from tripods. On the ground nearby were three water buckets. Buckets that would take longer to fill because the stream was farther away. But here, close at hand, on the strip of land sheltering them from the open sea, a fourth bucket. A bucket set far enough beyond a tree so that she tripped on it.

Four men? Bree wondered. *Not three? And the fourth man making sure that his water was used?*

ELEVEN

RUN!

B y the time they reached the Wicklow Mountains, both Keely and Lil had walked through the leather in their shoes. Yet they nearly skipped up the path where they could look down over the Glendalough [*Glendaloch*] Monastery. Devin watched every expression that crossed Keely's face.

More than ninety-eight feet high, the round tower with three-foot walls and a cone-shaped roof pointed to the heavens. Built of heavy stones placed one on top of another, the tower seemed strong enough for almost anything. But Keely looked upon it with sadness.

"When I was little, I thought it would keep me safe," she said. "Now—"

Devin waited.

"Now I know what really counts." A light came into Keely's face, replacing her sadness. "What matters is that Jesus is with me."

For a moment longer they stood there, taking in the view below. The small prayer huts with straw roofs. The building where monks copied the Bible, letter by letter. The shining water of the upper and lower lakes.

Even from this distance the sounds of the monastery rose to them. A dog barked, a cow mooed, and men in long brown robes hurried here and there.

"Brother Cronan?" Keely asked as if reaching far back in memory. Not only did he teach at the monastery, he was a close friend of the family.

"Still there," Devin told her.

Lil linked her arm with Keely's. "Now the tower welcomes us home," Lil said. "Let's go!"

As though entering a race, they started to run, and Devin kept with them. Eager again, they passed through the forest and slowed down only when they came to the river. There they stopped and with great ceremony crossed over. On the other side, Devin opened the gate in the stone fence.

But Keely stopped. "I'm almost afraid to go back. What if it's not what I remember? Maybe Mam and Daddy won't recognize me."

"They will," Devin said.

"What if they don't love me anymore?"

Devin laughed. "Keely, you're a birdbrain. Get along with you, now." Taking her hand, he urged her up the path.

In that moment, Aidan O'Toole passed through the doorway of the cottage and stepped out into the sunlight. Suddenly Keely broke into a run.

"Daddy! Daddy!"

At the sound of her voice, her father ran to meet her. As his arms closed around her, Keely's feet swung off the ground. Around and around in circles her father swung her, as though unwilling to ever let her go.

They were still whirling when Maureen O'Toole stepped out of the doorway. "Aidan O'Toole, are you daft? Whatever is going on?"

And then, as she understood, Mam ran to Keely. When her daddy set Keely down, Mam threw her arms around her. Their tears came in such a flood it seemed as if they wet the earth itself.

When her brother and sisters lined up, waiting for their own hugs, Keely looked at them with puzzlement in her eyes. Though Bree and Devin had told her about them, she still needed to fit the faces and names together.

Adam stood there with the solemn, responsible look of an eight-year-old. "You're Adam, all grown up," Keely said, and her short brother grew taller.

But Keely needed help with the girls. Born after the

Vikings took Keely away, she hadn't known about them until Bree found her. "Cara," Mam told her, and a five-year-old with curly red hair stepped forward.

"And your newest sister, Jen." Jen was four now and shyer than the others. For a moment she hung back, not knowing what to do, but Keely's hug surrounded her.

Word about Keely's return spread quickly to the nearby cottages. One neighbor after another arrived, bearing food, good wishes, hugs, smiles, and laughter.

Then Devin remembered. "Run!" he said to the fastest young boy he knew. "Run for Lil's family. Tell her cousin Tully that Lil is here."

KING OLAF

That night Bree lay awake. *Who spoiled the soup?* she asked herself, trying to call up the face of each man.

Mikkel was right. It had to be done with water from the sea. If he couldn't find the person, she would. She would also keep close watch on everything she and Nola cooked.

The next day the *Sea Bird* and the *Conquest* left the Norwegian Sea and sailed inland. Near a winding loop in the river Nidelva, Bree saw a marketplace, houses, and fences. Streets were built with logs laid one against another. As they passed the buildings owned by merchants, Bree looked ahead to a piece of land jutting out into the river.

A harbor lay in the curve of the bay. Seeing it, Bree

wanted to know more about this town called Nidaros and the ships anchored at wide places in the river or in the bay.

Then Sigurd's men backpaddled, holding the *Sea Bird* in place. Ahead of them was the biggest ship Bree had ever seen.

"The *Long Serpent!*" As the *Conquest* drew close, Mikkel jumped up on his sea chest to look down inside the other ship. "Thirty-four rowing seats!" he exclaimed.

Bree knew that meant there were places for sixty-eight men to row. Mikkel turned to her. "Come here, Bree. You have to see this."

With his help she climbed up on a barrel. Not only were there more rowing seats than she had ever seen. The floorboards were specially carved. Gilding shone on the dragon figurehead and the crook at the stern.

"People say it's the best fitted, most costly ship ever built by Norwegians," Mikkel said. "And the king's fleet holds thirty ships!"

The excitement of seeing the *Long Serpent* passed from one man to the next. Guards stood in the ship and on the nearby land, watching all who came close. Bree soon realized that they had grown used to this kind of awe—the respect of seagoing men who knew a ship's true worth.

When Sigurd gave the signal to move on, he and Mikkel drew their ships up on shore. Above the harbor, the land rose to a house large and fine enough for a king. One of the king's men came forward.

"I am Sigurd, chieftain of the Aurland Fjord," Mikkel's father told him. "I seek an audience with King Olaf Tryggvason [*Trigvason*]. Would it be possible to talk with him?"

As Mikkel joined them, Sigurd turned. "My son, Mikkel. May he come with us?"

"I will bring greetings from both of you," the man answered formally. "When I return, I will tell you the king's wishes."

The moment the young man left, men from the *Sea Bird* and *Conquest* set up tents on the shore. Others carried firewood from the ships and heated water.

A short time later, when Sigurd and Mikkel emerged from their tents, they had bathed and combed their hair. Both of them wore their finest clothing.

Bree had never seen either of them so carefully dressed. Always they had been neat and clean at the start of the day. But both of them worked outside with their men. Now they wore soft leather boots instead of work shoes. Each wore a cloak of the finest cloth and carried a richly ornamented sword at his side.

Instead of his usual flyaway look with hair blown every direction by the wind, Mikkel's hair was carefully combed. Every strand was in place.

When Mikkel caught Bree staring, he grinned. "My mother always told me I clean up well."

A ripple of laughter flowed through Bree. "The people of Ireland should see you now."

But Mikkel did not laugh. When a flush crept into his tanned face, he looked away. Bree wished she could bite her tongue, but it was too late.

Soon the king's man returned. With him came a tall and strong man so impressive in appearance that Bree wondered if he was King Olaf himself. As he reached Sigurd, the tall man bowed formally before him.

"I am Leif Erikson of Greenland. The king wishes to see you at once."

Just as formally Sigurd nodded. "We are ready."

Turning, Leif led them away from the *Sea Bird*. Shoulders back, heads high, Sigurd and Mikkel walked side by side behind him.

Leif Erikson took them up a stone path to the large house set above the harbor. Only when Sigurd and Mikkel disappeared did Bree and the others start talking.

"He said he was Leif Erikson?" Garth asked. "He has to be the son of Erik the Red."

Long ago, Erik had been outlawed from Iceland because of crimes he committed. During the three years he was not allowed to set foot in his own country, he found and explored a new land.

Giving it the attractive name of Greenland, Erik returned to Iceland and organized a group of settlers.

Though twenty-five ships set out, only fourteen reached Greenland safely.

❀

Later that day a strangely quiet Mikkel told Bree about his audience with the king. When Mikkel found her, she was washing clothes in the river. To Bree's surprise Mikkel spoke only to her, as if he wanted her to know. But first he looked around, making sure that no one else heard.

"King Olaf is like my father," Mikkel began. "Both of them have the authority to rule. The king knows how to receive help from his friends and be careful of those who oppose him."

"And your father?" Bree asked. "How did he fare?"

"He told his story well. When he said it was the Christian God who healed him, a glad light came into King Olaf's eyes. He questioned my father about all that had happened and wanted to hear even the smallest detail of the story again."

"And King Olaf? Did you like him?"

"To my surprise I did. He is tall and handsome, taller than any other person I know. He is manly in appearance in much the same way as the Greenlander Leif Erikson. The king has faced greater foes. He has learned to use his power to rule. But—"

Mikkel's eyes were troubled.

"But what?" Bree asked.

"More than once I've heard stories about the king. Those who want to worship the gods we have always known oppose him strongly. Sometimes he meets those people well and leads them to his new belief. But other times—"

"Yes. Other times—" Bree remembered the uneasiness she felt on the voyage here as she heard the stories told around the fire. More than once she realized that King Olaf opposed pagan practices that were harmful to people. Sometimes he faced violent men who made heathen sacrifices. When she heard such stories, she began to understand. But Bree still wondered about other things the king did.

"Other times the king seems cruel," Mikkel told her. "It's like he's trying too hard."

Bree shivered. Leaning back, she looked toward the king's house, to his fleet of ships, and his *Long Serpent*. She had hoped the king would influence Mikkel for good. Instead, just the opposite seemed to have happened.

Finally Bree said, "It's the year one thousand. Does the king believe the world will end this year? Does he want everyone to become a Christian before that happens?"

"I don't know." Mikkel looked off down the river, as if finding it impossible to explain the rest. When at last he turned back, his eyes showed his pain.

"Bree, I see how my mother, and father, and grandparents are starting to know your God. I see how you and Devin live. In many ways it would be good to know your God."

"Yes," Bree said quietly. "It is."

"But how can I believe in something that causes a king to act the way he does? You don't like the way I live. Sometimes I don't treat people well. Why should I believe in your God if knowing Him won't help me change into someone better?"

"Oh!" The word was a gasp. Then Bree realized it was a moan. A moan that came from the very center of her heart. Tears came to her eyes, and she could not hold them back.

When Mikkel stared at her, she struggled to speak. "Mikkel, you understand that I'm not perfect?"

To her relief Mikkel grinned. "I have no doubt about that. You express your dislike of me quite often."

But Bree did not smile. She knew that this might be the most important thing she ever said to him. "No matter how much I'd like to be like my God, I don't always manage."

"Sometimes you're civil." Mikkel was teasing now, as though trying to comfort her. "You won't ever improve?"

"Maybe a little," Bree admitted. "But not as much as you'd like."

Again Mikkel grinned, but Bree would not stop. She had to say this while she could. "King Olaf isn't perfect either. Sometimes his old ways, his Viking habits, come through."

Mikkel nodded. Clearly he could agree with that.

"He's a strong leader and wants to use his power. I think he wants to unite your people. But that doesn't mean he always lives the way Jesus lived."

"Jesus?"

"My God. The person who died for my sins. When people did something wrong, He told them about it. They knew how He felt about what they did, but—"

Suddenly Bree couldn't go on. Swallowing hard, she had to speak around the lump in her throat. "But God loves me, Mikkel. He loves me the way I am. He wants to give me a heart of courage."

❁

In the days that followed, King Olaf often called for Sigurd. More than once Bree wondered what they talked about. She knew one thing. Mikkel's father was very wise.

Yet with each day that passed Bree grew more and more impatient. If they didn't leave soon, they would miss her brother when he returned to the settlement surrounded by seven mountains. *If we're not there at the right time, how will I ever find Dev again?*

One day as Bree washed cooking pots in the river, someone let Shadow off his walrus hide rope. By the time Bree saw him, he was far up the slope.

Bree hurried after him, but Shadow saw her coming. Leaping away, he raced toward the king's house. When Bree reached out for him, Shadow streaked around a corner. As Bree followed, the dog circled a woman carrying a large basket and slipped through an open door.

Inside, the hall was dark and quiet. After the sunlight, Bree blinked. Far down the hallway, Shadow stopped at a doorway. Through its opening, Bree saw a room large enough to seat an army. Shadow was only one step away from going in.

On tiptoes Bree crept closer and closer. Heart in her throat, she knew that in one instant all could be lost. But Shadow was so busy looking at what was in the room that he did not turn. Suddenly Bree pounced.

As the dog wiggled to get free, Bree held him with every ounce of strength she possessed. "Quiet, Shadow," she whispered in his ear. "Good dog, quiet."

When at last the dog lay still in her arms, Bree risked a quick look into the room.

Only two men sat at the long, narrow table. Bree recognized one of them—the man named Leif Erikson. Without doubt the other man was King Olaf himself.

"It is your intention to leave for Greenland soon?" he asked, as though they had talked about this before.

"It is my intention," Leif answered. "If the king is willing."

"You are to go there on a mission for me, to preach Christianity."

Leif nodded. "It is for the king to decide. But you know my father. I firmly believe it will be difficult to be a Christian missionary in Greenland."

But the king would hear none of it. "Don't be dismayed. There is no man better fitted for the task than you. You will have success."

"That can only be if I am supported by your protection."

"I'll send a priest and a Scottish couple with you. If you need their help, they run as fast as deer."

Just then Shadow wiggled again. With all her strength Bree held him to her chest. As Bree heard steps behind her, she whirled around to face Mikkel.

She had seldom seen him so angry. Taking her arm, he led Bree away from the open door. Once safely outside, he started walking fast and dragged Bree along with him. They were halfway to his ship, mingling with people in the marketplace, before Mikkel slowed down.

Looking around, he pulled Bree to one side where no one else could hear.

There he exploded. "What on earth were you doing in the king's house?"

"Getting Shadow."

Mikkel stared at her. "Getting a *dog?* Don't you know

you passed the guards surrounding the king? Don't you understand how serious that *is?*"

"No one stopped me," Bree said.

"Well, they should have. The king has enemies."

Enemies, Bree thought. *And who untied the rope holding my dog?* But then she forgot her question as she faced Mikkel's anger.

"The king has enemies that could enter his house just the way you did."

Enemies. Bree had no doubt that every leader had enemies. King Olaf seemed to have some especially strong ones. But for the first time Bree wondered if Mikkel had enemies of his own. Whatever he took on, Mikkel always seemed to succeed. Was there someone who wanted to get even?

Now Mikkel lowered his voice. "You know I don't like some of the things our king does."

"Nor do I." Without thinking, Bree spit out her words.

Mikkel glared at her. "You, a slave, would dare to speak against our king?"

Totally angry now, Bree forgot to be careful. "Not even God forces us to love Him. He gives us a choice."

"Shhhh!" Mikkel warned, glancing around. "If the king hears what you said—"

But Bree was so upset she could not be quiet. "Stop looking at people, and start looking at God!"

The moment the words escaped her lips, Bree saw heads turn. Mikkel grabbed her arm and moved her along. But he took a roundabout way back to the ship, and looked over his shoulder often.

TULLY'S QUESTION

In less time than Devin ever thought possible, his best friend Tully appeared at the door. His face was flushed from running, and his blond hair flew in all directions. In the nine months since Devin had seen him, Tully had grown up.

Then, as he looked around the room, Devin knew that the boy who carried the message to Lil's family had not warned Tully about Bree.

From one person to the next his gaze darted. When he saw Keely, a question came into his eyes. Then Tully's cousin Lil ran up to him.

Tully opened his arms and gave her a hug that lifted the young girl off the floor. When he set her down again, he said, "Your mam and daddy and all your brothers and sisters are on the way here!"

Then Tully stood back. A merry grin lit his face. "Ah, child. You are lookin' good. Those Vikings didn't hurt you none?"

Lil's grin matched his. "They would have hurt me here." Lil put her hand over her heart. "But I've been with Bree."

"Bree." Once again Tully looked around. Again his gaze fell on Keely. This time she noticed.

Her eyes darkened with sadness as she explained. "Bree gave me her place. She sent me home."

"She sent you home?" Tully blurted out. The disappointment of it spread across his face.

"I'm sorry, Tully," Keely said quickly. "You thought you'd see Bree, didn't you?"

"No, no, that's not it," Tully said quickly. "I'm just surprised. It's so good to see you home after all these years. I can't believe Dev found you."

But Keely turned away, and after a moment Tully followed her. "Keely," he said firmly, apology in his voice. "I made a mistake, but Bree was right."

"She was right in sending me home?" Tears filled Keely's deep brown eyes. "It's Bree you're missing. I can't make up for that."

"You don't have to. It's seven years now since you were snatched away. Bree knew that all of us have prayed for you every one of those livelong days. Bree knew your comin' home would be an answer to our prayers."

"Really?"

"As sure as I stand in front of you. And Bree knew *you* needed to be home."

"How did she know that, Tully? What do you mean?"

"Bree is a wise one, that girl is. She knows that every girl needs to be with her mam and daddy, and you've missed a lot of that. Now go and get as many hugs from them as you can."

When Keely smiled, it was like seeing a pot of gold at the end of an Irish rainbow. "Thank you, Tully," she said softly.

But Devin reached Tully before he could say another word. "Let's go for a walk," Devin said.

Down the path they went through the forest to the place where stepping-stones led across the river. Only then did Tully speak. "I thought you'd bring Bree back! All this time, and she's still not with you!"

"I know." Dev spoke quietly.

Tully faced him. "Dev, you have to tell me. How is Bree doing? Was she hurt? What's happening to her?"

Without realizing it, Tully dropped down on the rock where Mikkel had stood before falling into the water. Devin sat on another rock nearby. With the sound of water tumbling around the stones, Devin told his story.

"What went wrong?" Tully asked when Devin

described the fjord where Bree lived. "Why didn't she come home?"

When Devin explained, Tully spoke again. "Is there some reason Bree wants to stay there?"

"No." Devin faced his friend head-on. "She knew the younger girls needed to come home even more than she did."

Only then could Tully understand. "Yes, that's the way Bree is. But what will happen now?"

"I'll go back—"

"No, I'll go—"

"You?"

Tully glared at him. "*Me.* What's wrong with me going?"

Devin stared at him. "Mikkel grabbed the ransom I brought. Men took me, put me in a hole in the ground they called a jail. What's to stop them from doing the same to you?"

But Tully wouldn't listen.

"You don't know the people," Devin said. "You wouldn't know what you'd be walking into—who to trust, who to fear—"

Tully broke into his words. "Who is this Mikkel, anyway?"

Devin met his gaze. "Someone who looks much like you. The day before the Vikings came, Bree saw him here. She thought you were the one who fell into the water. She thought she was rescuing you."

As Tully shook his head at the strangeness of it, Devin went on. "He looks much like you, but there's a big difference. You are kind. You care about Bree—"

Devin stopped. Suddenly it struck him. Always he had thought of Mikkel as cruel—greedy. *Greedy, yes.* That's what had started this whole thing. And more than once Devin had seen how Mikkel wanted to make a big name for himself. *Ambitious.*

But cruel? Devin honestly couldn't say that Mikkel was cruel. When had he changed? And now Tully was waiting for him to explain.

"Not cruel," Tully said, a strange light in his eyes. "And not dirty. Not the dirty stinking Vikings from the North."

"How did you know?" Devin blurted out, and his words made Tully even more angry.

"They're clean," he said. "Someone told me. They use combs and bathe and trim their beards and—"

"Yes." And now Devin knew what was wrong. "You don't have to worry," he said. "Bree will never love Mikkel."

"You're my friend," Tully answered. "My very best friend. You wouldn't lie to me?"

"No. She hates him."

"Hates him?"

"Well, she keeps forgiving him, but—"

Tully looked away. Without speaking he stared at the

clear water flowing past the first stepping-stone into the stream.

"Bree loved the sound of water," he said finally. "She loved hearing water spill over rocks, coming down our mountainsides."

His words frightened Devin. The way Tully spoke, it was as if Bree had died. Devin refused to let Bree die, not even in his thoughts. But what could he say? What if he gave Tully hope that Bree would return and the hope never became real?

Suddenly Tully turned to Devin. "Dev, how can we set it all straight? What can I do?"

For some time they talked about one plan, then another. Finally they stopped. Neither of them could come up with a plan that gave Tully something to do.

As Tully started to weep, Devin put his arm around his shoulders. "Tully, there's something I want you to know. Bree cried when she heard your name."

❦

It was late at night before the last of the neighbors left and Devin could talk with his parents. Because his father was a chieftain, their cottage was bigger than most. Along one side of the large open room, high walls went most of the way to the ceiling. The walls created a row of small rooms, each with a bed. Keely was back in the room she knew as a six-year-old, but this time she shared it with Cara and Jen.

Pulling up their low benches, Aidan, Maureen, and Devin sat before the fire. With the night quiet around them, Devin took a deep breath. "When I was in jail, I dreamed I could smell a peat fire."

His mother had the same questions as Tully. Was Bree hurt? What happened to her? Was she all right?

To his mam and daddy, Devin answered as he had for Tully. "Bree's tough, you know. Tougher than I ever thought her."

"Not tough," Mam said. "Strong."

"Yes, strong." Devin smiled.

"Strong in the Lord?" Aidan asked.

"Strong in the Lord. Whatever happens, Bree will be all right."

But Aidan pounced on his words. "Whatever happens? What do you mean?"

Fear leaped into Maureen's eyes. "Isn't Bree coming home?"

When Devin explained what Bree had done to ransom Keely and Lil, his parents grew quiet. "You have to go back?" Mam asked at last.

Unable to speak, Devin nodded.

Aidan's anger spilled out. "Why?"

When Devin explained about Mikkel's promise to free Bree after one voyage, his parents sat with the weight of it upon them. As they stared into the fire, the silence grew long between them.

Finally Mam spoke. "You cannot go back, Devin."

When he stared at her, she said it again. "You cannot go back."

"But—" Devin looked to his father.

Within Aidan's eyes Devin saw the same regret. "This Mikkel—"

This time Devin knew what the question would be. "I don't understand why, but I trust him to take care of Bree."

But Aidan O'Toole, mighty chieftain in the Wicklow Mountains, spoke from his long experience with people. "If you go, and Mikkel changes his mind—"

Aidan snapped his fingers. "Both of you are lost to us forever."

Devin waited, knowing his father spoke truth.

"You said that Bree has not been harmed—"

"So far."

"She has not been harmed." Aidan's words were firm, but his eyes were upon his wife. "And we all know that Bree knows how to take care of herself. If she managed to escape, could she find her way home?"

"With the Lord's help," Devin said.

"Ahhhh." For the first time since their talk began, Aidan smiled. "You have grown, my son. The Lord's iron has been forged within you. Forged through hardship?"

Devin nodded, grateful for his father's words. "Forged within a smithy shop, making rivets for a Viking ship. Forged within a hole in the ground, the jail in which I lived. But forged most of all by knowing that Bree was lost to our family. I need to go back."

"Why?" Aidan's question shot out like an arrow.

"Because of Mikkel's promise. If I am there, he will have to set my sister free."

"If you are not?"

Devin didn't answer. He didn't want to even think about it. How could he live with himself if he didn't go back? How could Bree live—waiting, waiting, waiting for him to return?

"Don't go back," Ingmar had said. "Do you trust Mikkel?"

"Don't go back for the coins," Bjorn had told him. "It's not worth it."

Don't go back. The words whirled around in Devin's mind. *Don't go back.*

Devin looked to his father, then his mother. "If I return, I must meet Ingmar's ship in Dublin fourteen days from the time he let me off."

"Twelve days from now," his father said.

Devin nodded. "If God wants me to go back, He will show you."

"Let's pray," Aidan said.

Seated before the dying fire, his mother on one side,

his father on the other, Devin bowed his head. But his heart beat out one thought. *I have to go back. I need to help Bree.*

FOURTEEN

WHERE'S DEVIN?

That evening Mikkel started asking questions again. He and Sigurd sat apart from the others where they could talk without being overheard. As Bree served them food, Sigurd turned to her. "What do *you* say about some of the things King Olaf is doing?"

"I say what my daddy taught me." It seemed strange to Bree that a man as wise as Sigurd should ask her, a slave, what she thought. But now he leaned forward, as though he really wanted to know.

"And what did your father teach you?"

"He said, 'I became a Christian in a moment. But I'll spend my whole life learning to live the way Jesus did.'"

"Yes." Sigurd's eyes were thoughtful. "That's what

God was trying to show me, wasn't it? He loved me even before I knew Him. I didn't understand what that love is."

Listening to Sigurd, Bree remembered a question she'd had for a long time. "Why did you name Mikkel after a mighty prince?"

Sigurd smiled. "Because that's what I want him to be. When I was a trader in Dublin, I heard about the Michael in your Bible."

Mikkel looked startled. "I'm named after a prince?"

"A high-ranking angel," Bree told him. "The prince who protects God's people."

But Mikkel was not pleased. "Protect God's people? That's not my job," he told his father. "Why do you want me to do that?"

"You can't by yourself." Sigurd turned to Bree. "Is it true that your Jesus was not only a king but also a servant?"

A twinkle lit Sigurd's eyes. When Bree nodded her yes, she wanted to laugh. One look at Mikkel, and she decided she better not.

Then Sigurd told Mikkel, "King Olaf has asked that I stay with him for a time. You must sail to Iceland without me."

Mikkel stared at his father. "We planned on going together."

"I'm disappointed too. As soon as I can leave, I'll try to find you."

Suddenly Bree felt relieved. Maybe they could still meet Dev in time. If they didn't, she might never find him.

Mikkel looked upset. He liked sailing with his father. On the ocean it was also safer to have more than one ship. But now?

"Be first out of the harbor in the morning," Sigurd told him.

"Why?"

Meeting his son's gaze, Sigurd glanced at Bree. "Get ready tonight," he told Mikkel. "In the morning, don't delay."

Listening to him, Bree felt uncomfortable. Had someone told Sigurd what she said about King Olaf?

Mikkel asked no more questions. As he said goodbye, Mikkel stood straight and strong before his father. Watching Mikkel, Bree tried to tell herself that he wasn't afraid to lead this voyage on his own. With his shoulders squared and head high, the courage in his heart seemed to shine through his face. But there was something—

What is it? Bree wondered. *What is it?*

Then Sigurd spoke once more to Mikkel. "You must take Bree home. Do what you can to set right the wrong you have done."

Mikkel stiffened, but Sigurd waited. Finally Mikkel met his father's eyes and nodded.

"Briana," Sigurd said, and Bree felt surprised he knew

her real name. "When more of us believe in the Christian God, the raids will end."

Bree stared at him. Though Sigurd was always wise, his words seemed impossible to believe.

"You know better than any of us what that will mean," he said.

When Bree nodded, Sigurd's gaze held hers. "I'm sorry for the suffering of your people."

In the silence that followed, Mikkel stood without moving, watching his father walk away.

❀

While staying in the king's town, Bree had learned that the people living even farther north enjoyed continual daylight from mid-May through July. Now, in Nidaros, during the brief dusky hours when the midnight sun didn't give as much light, Mikkel's men took up their oars.

As they slipped out of the harbor and down the winding river, they made no sound. In the still hours of very early morning, they rowed through a channel into the Norwegian Sea.

Wind filled the sail, and Bree saw Mikkel take a deep breath. Yet all that day and the next he turned often to study the sea behind him.

When at last the *Conquest* passed between a line of rocky islands and the higher land of the coast, Bree knew where she was. Soon the body of water widened into the large open area surrounded by seven mountains. There they were to meet Devin.

Mikkel's men pulled the ship onto shore, and Bree climbed down to look around. Nola met her eyes. Both of them knew how much the Irish had suffered here. Newly captured, each of them had wondered what lay ahead. Where they would go. How they would be treated.

"I never thought I'd be here again," Bree whispered.

"Nor I. Sure, and if it doesn't look just the same."

But to Bree it didn't. Looking up, she felt as if she knew every step of the steep mountainside.

"Nola," she asked. "Did you meet Garth on the trip from Ireland?"

Nola shook her head. "He wasn't along. He would have kept Mikkel from making the raid."

Bree sighed. With all her heart she wished Garth had been along. But it also bothered her.

Strange, she thought. Why did she feel that she knew Garth and Hammer before seeing them at the farm?

"Your brother will come," Nola said now. "You will be together." For an instant Nola's gaze rested on her husband.

"You're happy, aren't you?" Bree wanted to ask more, but Mikkel called to her.

"Devin isn't here!"

Already Bree had looked from one merchant ship to

the next, hoping to find Ingmar. "They're just a bit late," she told Mikkel.

But the next morning Devin was not there. All day and into the evening he was not there. During the next two days, her brother still did not come.

On the fourth morning when the light of day crept above the eastern mountains, Bree watched the reflection in the water. Then she washed her face, combed her hair, and brushed the wrinkles out of her clothing. But nothing could take the wrinkles from her heart.

"Please, God," she prayed again. "Please bring Dev."

"I'm sorry, Bree," Mikkel said that morning. "We don't have any choice but to leave."

"Dev will come," she told him. "I know he will come."

"Maybe he decided to not come back."

Bree looked away, unable to face that possibility. *What if Dev didn't reach Ingmar's ship on time? What if Mam and Daddy said it was too big a risk? Worse still, what if Ingmar's ship went down at sea?*

"Can we wait one more day?" she asked.

When Mikkel shook his head his eyes were kind, but his words did not change. "We might wait forever, and he doesn't come."

"But what if he comes, and we're not here? I might never see Dev again."

"That's true. I'm sorry."

Mikkel turned to Nola. "Get everything together. We're leaving at once."

With quick steps Mikkel stalked over to his tent. Faster than Bree dreamed possible, he took it down. The *Conquest* was ready to go before Bree could believe they were leaving.

As the men pushed off, Bree stood at the stern with her back to the large dragonhead at the bow. Between one western island and the next they sailed. And then Bree turned, making herself face the dragon and the open sea.

FIFTEEN

THE DREAM

As one day followed another, Devin grew more and more frantic inside. Each time his parents questioned him, he tried to tell them that Bree was all right. He didn't want to make his parents worry. But he also wanted them to understand that Bree needed his help.

Each day Tully came over or Devin walked to his house. But Devin knew that none of the plans they had talked through were right. Much as Tully wanted to rescue Bree, Devin alone had built trust with Mikkel. He alone knew all the ways that Mikkel could change his mind and Bree's life.

On the tenth day, Devin gathered all that he needed for the trip in a cloth bag. On the eleventh day, he talked to his father where his mother could not hear. "If I don't set out soon, I'll miss Ingmar's ship."

"He's a Viking you trust?" Aidan asked for at least the fifteenth time.

"A Norwegian I trust," Devin replied. "He's a kind young man. He's like Bjorn—the Norse cobbler who trades with you."

On the evening of the eleventh night, Devin went to bed with despair in his heart. He had counted every hour that it took to walk to Dublin. Even if he ran as often as possible, he could barely make it. If he did not leave before first light—

Troubled at heart, Devin fell asleep while still praying. He woke to sobbing in the night. At first Devin didn't understand what he heard. Then he knew the weeping came from his father and mother's room.

Dressing quickly, Devin went out to the hearth. Banked for the night, the embers were hidden by ashes, but Devin still felt their warmth. Drawing a bench close, he waited, still praying. Finally the door to his parents' room opened.

"I thought I'd find you here," his father said.

When he led Devin's mother out, she huddled within a blanket. Devin soon knew she was not shrinking away, but gathering strength to speak.

"I dreamed this night," she said as she took another stool. "The dream made me afraid, for I saw Bree in a great Viking ship. The wind was full in the sail, and the waves rose high around the railings. The darkness was great upon them, but Bree stood at the bow of the ship. A man dressed in white stood beside her.

"I cried out, afraid of the storm, the waves, and the darkness. Afraid for Bree. But then the darkness disappeared, and light fell upon the white robe of the man. I knew words I learned long ago. 'Take courage,' He said. 'It is I. Don't be afraid.'

"When I stopped crying, I sensed something else. Has God called Bree to be a light to the nations?"

When Devin could not answer, his mother went on. "Then the light faded. The man in white was gone, but you, Devin, were standing next to Bree."

For a moment Mam stopped and pushed back her reddish blond hair that was the same color as Bree's. Then Mam spoke again.

"You must go, Devin. I don't understand why, but I know that you must be with her. And one day, you'll come home together."

Devin stared at his mother. "You are giving me permission to go?"

"To go to Bree," his father answered. "Find her. Stay with her. Help her."

"But it may be a long time before we get back."

"We know. God will tell us by the peace in our hearts how you are doing."

Standing up, Devin hugged his mother. "Don't go without saying good-bye to the others," she said.

Together the three of them went to each room. Adam woke easily, and the others were more sleepy. But each of them understood. In the morning Devin would be gone. And it would be a long good-bye.

SIXTEEN

WHALES!

As Mikkel's ship passed the outermost island, Bree heard it. At first she thought she was imagining the music.

A panpipe.

Once before, Bree had heard that high clear sound when she thought all was lost. Now, afraid to believe, Bree swung around.

There it was. A ship growing larger all the time. A mighty sail filled with wind, making full speed their way. A ship with someone playing the bright, quick notes of an Irish song. A song that told Bree her brother was coming.

"Mikkel!" she cried. "He's here!"

But Mikkel had already ordered the sail to be lowered. Taking up oars, the men headed toward Ingmar's ship. Bree hurried forward. Beneath the dragonhead she stood with tears streaming down her cheeks. Only when Mikkel called out to Devin did Bree wipe her face.

When Ingmar's ship came alongside, men reached out, holding the two ships together. Standing next to Devin, Ingmar clapped his shoulder and spoke one last word. Then he turned to Bree.

Stretching out his hand, Ingmar reached across the space between them. A glad light filled his eyes. "Your sister and friend are safe at home," he said. "But your brother refused to stay there."

For a moment Ingmar's gaze met Bree's eyes. "When you are ready to go home, I will take you and Devin to Dublin."

"No!" Mikkel exclaimed. "You will *not* take them to Ireland!"

Bree swung around. Seeing the anger in his eyes, she felt anger of her own. "You promised I could go home!"

"I promised that I would set you free. I did not promise that Ingmar would take you home."

Turning to Devin, Mikkel spoke quickly. "Your sea chest?"

Men passed it between them and set it down in Mikkel's ship.

"You're ready?" Mikkel's gaze met Devin's, but the words were a challenge.

"I'm ready," he said, but the fierce light in his eyes did not give in to Mikkel. "I'm ready if you treat Bree and me fairly."

Mikkel straightened. "I am Mikkel, son of Sigurd, mighty chieftain of the Aurland Fjord."

"And I am Devin O'Toole, son of—"

To Bree's surprise her brother stopped midsentence. Then she remembered. Always it was at the same point that she herself stopped, held back as surely as if someone clapped a hand over her mouth. Held back from telling Mikkel that she was the daughter of a mighty chieftain.

Then Bree stretched out a hand, and the moment was gone. But Devin did not need Bree's help. Instead, he jumped from one ship to the next. When he landed on the deck of Mikkel's ship, he had his sea legs, as surely as any longtime sailor.

Quickly he turned back to Ingmar. "A hundred thousand thanks!" he called. "And when you come to Ireland—"

Ingmar nodded, as though he already knew the end of the sentence. For one moment he looked at Bree. As their gaze met, she smiled, giving her thanks. Then Ingmar gave the order to be off.

"Tully is upset," Devin told Bree when they were able to talk. All day long and through the evening, the *Conquest* had made good time across the North Atlantic. Now in the few hours of darkness Bree and her brother sat at the stern, talking so fast that their words spilled over.

Dev started by telling Bree about their parents. "Mam?" Bree had asked.

"She could hardly believe it when Keely walked up the path. Mam never gave up hope of seeing Keely again, not even after you were taken away. The whole time I was home she just kept saying, "Sure, and if finding Keely isn't a miracle straight from the hand of God.""

Bree smiled. "And Daddy?"

"He caught Keely up, danced her around the cottage and then the yard. When he finally saw me, he gathered me into that great big hug of his. When Keely and I were thoroughly smothered, unable to breathe, he finally let us go."

Together they went through each family member—Adam, Cara, and Jen. All of them were nearly a year older now. When Devin told how each of them wondered about her, Bree grew quiet.

"What did they want to know?" she asked.

"Where you lived, what your life was like, how people treated you."

"Yes, that's what they'd ask."

"And Mam asked, 'What's she like on the inside? Does she find any happiness?'"

Bree smiled. "That's Mam, all right." Bree waited, knowing without being told that Devin would speak of her daddy next.

When Devin answered he sounded like their father. "He said, 'And what does Bree believe about God by now?'"

Hearing Dev, Bree laughed. It was Daddy who had once walked away from the church and all that God meant. It was because of her father that Bree understood Mikkel and his questions.

"And, my good brother, what did you tell Daddy? What did you say I believed?"

"That at first you wondered about God's protection." Devin lowered his voice even more. "You asked why God allowed you to be stolen away by Vikings."

Suddenly Devin glanced over to where Mikkel stood, his hand on the tiller, looking off to sea. To Bree it looked as if Mikkel's ears were standing out from his head.

"And then," Devin went on in a quieter voice, "I told them what you told me. That you were starting to understand the reason."

In the darkness Bree still waited to hear about one more person.

"Tully's upset," Dev said again. "He misses you. He wants you home."

"I want to go home." Bree's voice reflected the longing of her heart.

More than once Mikkel told them they were making good time. If all continued to go well, they would make the crossing to Iceland in three or four days.

"Good," Bree told him. "When you sell your logs we can go home."

It seemed hard to believe her time of slavery was almost over. Much as she now liked to sail, she often thought about Mikkel's promise.

Hour after hour he stood at the bow looking ahead. At night he was the one most often taking the tiller. Often he smiled—smiled more than Bree had ever seen. It was as if Mikkel knew he was made for being the master of a ship. What's more, he loved this ship he had worked so hard to build. Each time Mikkel ran his hand along the rails, his eyes shone with pride.

Devin was little better. All winter long he had worked in the blacksmith shop on the farm. Month after month, he pounded pieces of iron, making countless rivets to hold the overlapping boards of the ship together. Now

Devin often bent over a rail, checking a rivet in the bright light of the sun.

In the wide north Atlantic, there seemed nothing between them and the distant heavens. No longer did Bree feel angry at being taken from her home. Yes, she would never lose her desire to go back. Yet in a strange way God was fulfilling her lifelong dream to see what lay beyond the mountains and the Irish Sea.

Bree had never guessed God would use this way to help her travel. After becoming a slave, she had told Him quite regularly that she didn't understand what He was doing. Now she had begun asking, *How can I be part of Your plan? Will You give me a heart of courage for whatever You want me to do?*

❀

One morning, as Bree lay on the deck of the Viking ship, she woke to the cry of seabirds. As she caught the scent of land, she forgot about the mysterious happenings that had never been explained. The fish soup spoiled with salt water. The dog, Shadow, let loose to enter the house of a king. The reason why Sigurd wanted them to leave Nidaros.

Yet something always lay unspoken and unresolved between Bree, Devin, and Mikkel. Everyone knew about the monastery gems, and Bree often wondered if there were men who wanted to steal them. After all, wouldn't

Mikkel have taken the gems along to use in trade if needed? But only Bree and Devin knew about the coins stolen from Sigurd's friend. Where had Mikkel managed to hide his treasure?

Soon a lookout high on the mast sighted land. Before long, the *Conquest* sailed with a thin line of land off to their right. Then Devin called to Bree. "Look!"

As Bree faced the front of the ship, she saw a long black shape off the port, or left side. Then she spotted a tall plume of water.

"There she blows!" cried one of the men. A moment later the whale dove deep beneath the surface.

Soon there were more whales, closer now to the ship. In the sunlight, water glistened on their great long backs. More than once, a large tail fin flipped up, then down, as it sent the whale forward through the water. Bree felt the excitement run through the ship.

Then as Bree glanced toward Mikkel, she felt something more. He, too, stared ahead, but his face was set, his eyes watchful as he scanned the sea.

Five or six whales were within sight. Some swam quietly. White froth and waves churned around others.

Uneasy thoughts crept into Bree's mind. A moment later they entered her heart. *What if?* she wondered. *What if?*

Until now the *Conquest* had seemed large. Compared to the whales, the ship suddenly looked very small. Bree moved along the rails until she stood next to her brother.

"Stay close," he warned. "Don't let anything separate us."

The words were barely out of Devin's mouth when the whales were gone. As the water settled, Bree felt relieved.

❀

We'll be in Iceland soon, Bree promised herself as the sun cast orange-gold light on the water. The voyage had gone well. A few more days and Mikkel would trade the logs stored in the center of the ship. Lying on both sides of the mast, they were lashed down and secure.

Before long, she and Devin could start home. As Bree put down her sleeping sack near the stern of the ship, her heart felt glad.

During the few short hours of darkness, she stirred in her sleep. As she wondered what awakened her, Bree sensed a movement. Rising up on her elbow, she looked around.

The man at the tiller had turned starboard, toward the steering board on the right side of the ship. As he looked off toward land, all was still. Moments after she lay down, Bree slept again.

In the morning a gray whale appeared on the port or left side as Bree faced forward. To her surprise the whale lingered near the ship, as though curious instead of afraid.

At first Bree thought the whale was alone. Then Devin came and stood with her at the rail.

"See the calf with its mother?" he asked. "Ingmar told me that a new mother often swims behind the rest. She needs to go slower so her calf can keep up."

The small whale swam close to its mother's side. At first Bree enjoyed watching them. Then she noticed a whale coming up quietly from behind. Black and glossy with a white underside, it had a raised center fin that stood high in the water.

Suddenly the mother increased her speed. But the black whale drew closer, and other black and white whales joined him. Soon they tried to get between the mother and her calf.

Filled with panic, the mother flipped her large tail fin, slamming it down with a mighty splash. As the wave caught the ship, the port side lifted.

Bree's heart lurched. As the deck slanted sharply beneath her, she grabbed hold of the rail. Then Devin grabbed hold of Bree. Arms linked, they clung to the rail and each other.

Suddenly a log broke loose, flying out of place. One log followed another, cracking with a loud thud against the starboard side. As the ship listed to starboard, more logs rolled. Across the top of sea chests they flew. Kegs, barrels, and chests followed the logs into the sea.

Men leaped to balance the ship, but it was too late. In the next instant someone cried, "Men overboard!"

With the deck almost straight up and down, Bree clung to the rail and her life. As more logs spilled out, the ship rocked back and forth. Rocked yet again, then held upright.

Logs still lay on the port side of the mast. The moment the ship settled, Devin and Bree hurried to the other side. In the water around them, sea chests and logs, barrels, and anything else that would float bobbed on the surface. Near the ship, two men thrashed the water with the desperate strokes that told Bree they didn't know how to swim.

When Devin threw out a rope weighted with a board, one of the men grabbed it. A second rope went to the other man, and both were pulled in.

One, two, three, four? Five people, Bree thought. Rowing desperately, oarsmen brought the ship to a man farther out. Hands reached down and pulled him on board. Two more men, both clinging to logs, were rescued last.

Then Bree saw Mikkel. The water was still full with all kinds of debris, but he stood counting his men. "Anyone missing?" he asked.

Teeth chattering, the rescued men huddled inside blankets. When everyone was accounted for, Mikkel walked over to the center of the ship. There he picked up the walrus hide ropes that had lashed down the logs.

When Bree saw Mikkel's face, she trembled. No longer did she wonder about the spoiled soup or Shadow let loose. Without doubt she knew that Mikkel felt certain that this was not an accident. Who hated him so much that he would do this terrible thing?

Working together, the men lifted one sea chest after another out of the water. Then came the kegs and barrels. Finally Mikkel said, "Let the logs wash in to shore."

As the *Conquest* drew close to land, another ship came near. Mikkel recognized its master. "Leif Erikson!"

"We'll help you!" Leif called out as he realized what had happened. Working together, the two crews collected the logs and loaded them on the *Conquest* again.

Though Mikkel seemed calm enough, one eye twitched. With his men standing before him, Mikkel held up the ropes that had lashed down the logs.

"Someone cut them," he said. Looking from one crew member to the next, Mikkel waited. Every man met his gaze.

"You know that our ship nearly capsized." As Mikkel spoke, his stern words held them with their power. "You know that we could have lost every person on board. I ask you who are innocent to bring the guilty to me."

SEVENTEEN

LAND OF FIRE AND ICE

"Come," Leif said to Mikkel when the *Conquest* was ready to sail again. "I'll show you where to bring your ship to shore."

Leif led them to a harbor filled with ships from many parts of the world. But the *Conquest* entered the Icelandic settlement of Reykjanes without answers to life-or-death questions. Bree felt troubled by all that had happened.

Salt water in the soup instead of fresh. A dog let loose to enter a king's house. Sigurd's warning to leave. And now, what could have been total disaster. Whoever was causing trouble, the person had to be part of the crew. But why? What motive did he have?

When Bree talked with Devin, their thoughts came down to one question. *Who wants to hurt Mikkel? And why?*

More than anyone, Bree knew how easy it was to hate him. Hadn't she herself often felt that way? Again and again, Bree needed to learn that God wanted her to forgive him. It was the only way she could deal with the pain she felt because Mikkel led the raid that took her from her family.

Now, strangely enough, Bree didn't feel that hate any more. It surprised her. *Did I forgive enough times so I finally don't hurt?* Yet she understood why someone might want to get even.

"Whoever did this hates Mikkel even more than I did," she whispered to Devin. "But you and Nola and I are the only Irish on this trip. Who hates Mikkel enough to put everyone, including himself, in danger?"

Devin put it plainly. "Who wants revenge? When we know that, we'll know who it is."

"Revenge." Bree shivered.

"Getting even. No matter what. Whatever it involves, it must be big."

Bree could only wonder about a mind so twisted that a man could threaten his own life in order to get revenge. From that time on, she watched and listened as she had never done before.

The moment Mikkel's men brought the *Conquest* up onshore, Leif Erikson walked over to talk. "Why don't you come with me to Greenland?" he asked Mikkel. "We're a land without the timber we need. You would earn an even bigger profit by selling your logs there."

Leif planned to attend the *Althing*, the annual meeting of Iceland's parliament. People came from all over the country, some of them traveling for two weeks in order to meet together. If Mikkel waited for the *Althing* to be over, he could simply follow Leif home.

As Mikkel listened to him, Bree felt a sinking deep inside. "No!" she cried out to Devin first, and then Mikkel.

"You promised," she told him when Leif left. "You promised that after one voyage you'd set me free. You said Dev and I can go home. Now you talk about going to Greenland?"

Mikkel grinned. "Just think, Bree. I probably can earn twice as much—maybe three or four times as much—just by taking the logs to Greenland. But I'm still thinking about what Leif said."

Mikkel's confidence was back. In spite of what he said, Bree felt sure he had already made up his mind.

Leaving some men to guard the ship, sea chests, and timber, Mikkel set out with others for the *Althing*. Bree and Devin walked nearby.

On that June morning, the path from the harbor was filled with people. Some were fortunate enough to have a horse and cart for carrying their food and tent. Others carried whatever they needed on their backs. But Bree soon noticed that the *Althing* was also a gathering of the wealthy and people from other lands.

Since its first annual assembly in 930, the *Althing* had met at Thingvellir [*Tingvelear*] every year. This year's gathering of the national parliament was an especially important one. People on two sides of an important issue had drawn up battle lines.

As Bree walked, she listened to the people around her. From nearby she heard two men, one on either side of the problem.

One man was among those who wanted to accept the religion of the king of Norway. Countless Icelandic settlers had come from there. Many still had deep roots and ties with family and friends.

And wouldn't it be an economic advantage to accept Christianity? For hadn't King Olaf himself promised to encourage trade if Iceland became a Christian nation? But more than that, many people had already taken on deeply held beliefs. Vikings with Irish wives had brought their strong faith to Iceland.

The other man refused to give up his pagan religion, including his belief in his favorite god Thor. "How can I leave all that I believe about Odin and the other gods?" he asked. "Wouldn't they be angry with me?"

As the argument grew more heated, the men raised their voices. Bree asked Mikkel to explain.

"They're saying, 'You're out of law with me.'" Mikkel spoke so quietly that only she and Devin could hear.

"They're out of law?" Bree asked. "What do they mean?"

"It's like saying, 'You're doing something contrary to law.' Iceland is a commonwealth—a self-governing free nation with leaders who make democratic decisions. But now people on the different sides want to go separate ways. If this arguing doesn't stop, there will be civil war."

By this time the two men were so angry that Bree wondered if they'd end their argument in a fight. Then one of the men asked, "You say that important Christians helped your son with King Olaf, even though Christians don't believe what you and your son believe?"

When the father nodded, both men fell silent.

❀

As Bree, Devin, and others from the *Conquest* drew close to the large open area called Thingvellir, the path became more and more crowded. Yet when Bree entered the broad plain, she felt a stillness within her.

It surprised her, for everywhere she looked, people were talking. Even so, Bree felt the quiet beauty of the tall, dark columns of hardened lava. She drank in the deep blue of the lake and the river that wound its way through the valley. Against the distant horizon lay white-capped mountains.

Some people had booths—small buildings built of stone and turf with a cloth roof. Bree suspected that many wealthy people used these from year to year. Other people carried boards and cloth to put up a tent. Still others spread a cloth on the ground, crawled into their sleeping sack, or lay down under their cloak.

Wherever she looked, Bree saw people facing the high, grass-covered area called the Law Rock. There the law speaker stood. Each year he recited one third of the laws from memory while people sat on the slopes, listening and learning.

When talk turned to the most important issue at hand, one speaker after another rose and voiced his concern. As one day passed into the next, the battle lines formed. On one side were Christians. On the other side, those believing in the Norse gods.

Soon Bree realized the men on the road reflected the intense feelings held by both sides. When tempers flared, Bree felt afraid of the anger she saw.

Finally a man rose, saying, "Good people of Iceland, we cannot continue this way. If we do not reach agreement, we will destroy our country. Since our first assembly in the year 930 we have mediated our differences. I propose that we choose an arbitrator—a man respected by both sides—to give us a recommendation."

"Ah, yes, it is the Icelandic way," exclaimed a man near Bree.

"But who can we trust?" asked another.

Soon the assembly came to agreement. Thorgeir [*Torgear*], the constitutionally elected law speaker, was chosen.

"He'll take our side," said a man near Bree. "He's a pagan himself."

But the man next to him felt just the opposite. "Thorgeir has strong ties with people who are Christians."

As the law speaker stood on the high rock before them, Bree saw the wisdom in each word he spoke. "If I make a decision, will you choose to abide by it?" Thorgeir asked.

"Yes, yes!" called the chieftains.

Again Thorgeir looked around. "You will choose to abide by my decision?"

"Yes, yes!" Chieftains from both sides agreed.

A third time Thorgeir asked. "Yes!" the cry came, stronger still. For how else could they escape civil war, one side against another?

It seemed clear that both sides believed their viewpoint would be upheld.

For part of a day and through the night, Thorgeir lay under his cloak and did not leave his booth.

During the time that Thorgeir was gone, Leif Erikson found Mikkel. They were still together when Thorgeir returned to the Law Rock.

Again the law speaker asked the two sides what they would do. "Those who choose Odin, when I give my decision, will you abide by it?"

"Yes!" the chieftains called out.

"Those who choose Christianity, when I give my decision, will you abide by it?"

"Yes!" came the promise.

Again Thorgeir looked from one side of the large assembly to the other. "Know this!" he warned. "It will prove to be true that if we divide the law, we also divide the peace."

In the silence that followed, Thorgeir waited. When all appeared to be in agreement about accepting what he decided, Thorgeir said, "Then will I speak. This is my decision. That Iceland should become a Christian nation."

One side cheered. The other side looked stunned.

In the midst of her relief, Bree glanced over to Mikkel. It wasn't difficult to see that he was angry. "How can Thorgeir make such a decision? He's a traitor to his own beliefs."

But Leif Erikson spoke quietly. "No, he isn't. My father taught me the ways of Thor. He taught me so well that I did not find it difficult to become a Christian. Thorgeir knows what it means to live as I have. He is a wise man and wants what is best for his people. No doubt he also wants peace."

In contrast to the bloodshed and war in Norway, the chieftains accepted Thorgeir's decision that Iceland should become a Christian nation. It was made a law that all people should become Christian and that those who were not yet baptized should be.

Some were baptized at once in the cold waters at the *Althing*. Others waited until they reached warm spring waters on the way home.

When they returned to their ships, Leif talked with Mikkel again. "We can use whatever timber you bring us. If you go with me now, you'll learn the way to Greenland and can set up trade between us."

As Leif got his ship ready, Bree and Devin also talked with Mikkel. "One voyage," they reminded him. "You promised one voyage."

Mikkel nodded. "This is still one voyage."

But Bree was upset. "Do you know what happened when Leif's father led settlers from Iceland to Greenland? They started with twenty-five ships. Only fourteen reached Greenland."

"I know," Mikkel said. "But we have you along to pray."

Devin stared at him. "Like a good luck charm. That's what my sister is—a good luck charm for you. One prayer, and she'll set everything right."

Devin was angry now—as angry as Bree had ever seen him. So was she. "Don't forget that our God is the God who rules the universe."

"I won't," Mikkel said. "In case that's true, I want you and Devin along. If we get in trouble, you can put a good word in the ear of your God."

"But you're forgetting something," Bree told Mikkel. "Our God wants the best for us. But if we deliberately do something stupid—something He doesn't want us to do —we have to live with what happens."

When Mikkel fell silent, Bree thought she had convinced him. But then he spoke again.

"You and Devin do the praying. I'll do the thinking. In my thinking I'm convinced that we should go. And remember—I am the master of this ship."

When the two ships were ready, filled once again with water and provisions, Leif gave Mikkel directions to Brattahlid, his father's farm in Greenland.

"If we stay together, you can follow me," Leif said as Bree and Devin stood near Mikkel. "If we lose sight of each other, know that we have a snow-clad mountain that can be seen far out at sea."

Mikkel nodded, his face solemn as he took in every word.

"You need to remember that there are icebergs on the way. A large part of Greenland is covered by an ice cap—

a thick layer of ice and snow. When ice breaks off from a glacier, it slides into the ocean and becomes an iceberg."

Again Mikkel nodded, as though sure that he could handle it. But Leif went on. "There's a powerful current along the east coast of Greenland. It carries huge masses of ice, as well as icebergs split from glaciers."

"I'll watch for them," Mikkel said.

But Leif shook his head. "You don't understand. The sun and the wind melt the top of an iceberg, but the bottom of an iceberg is under water. It melts more slowly. And you can't see it."

"The largest part is under the surface of the water? Reaching out to any ship that comes too close?"

Leif nodded. "That's a good way to put it. You have to sail far south of Greenland. Stay out of sight of land and avoid the drift ice."

Drift ice. Large chunks of ice that had broken off from a glacier to slide into the sea.

"And of course, we also have storms and fog. If you miss the southern tip of Greenland—"

Having given the necessary warning, Leif grinned. "I strongly suspect that my father called it Greenland because a good name helps people want to come to a place."

"And it's green?" Mikkel asked.

Leif's laugh sounded as if he found a joke in it. "You'll see."

Though Leif was seven or eight years older, he and Mikkel already seemed friends. As Bree listened to them, she felt the tension within her growing.

To Bree it sounded impossible to reach Greenland safely. And they still faced another problem. Who on board the *Conquest* wanted to get even with Mikkel?

EIGHTEEN

FOREVER LOST?

As Mikkel stood at the tiller of the *Conquest,* he felt more worried than he wanted to admit. Then he remembered. In Greenland he would get the best price for his logs. If he established trade with the people there . . .

Mikkel smiled, just thinking about it. That's how fortunes were made. And when he overcame danger, he'd receive praise from others. Stories about his mighty deeds would be told in the great halls of the North. *Fame and fortune.*

Again Mikkel smiled. The tiller he held was smooth and well crafted. When he started building, he had hoped his new ship would surpass the *Sea Bird.* It had. By now he liked the *Conquest* even more. Fleet. Swift. Strong in appearance and strong in the open sea.

Now the sail billowed out, filled with wind. Already his fine ship had helped him overcome obstacles. He had named it well. He would indeed be a conqueror. An overcomer. One of the great Vikings.

For a moment Mikkel's gaze rested on Bree and Devin. Though they had tried their best to keep him from going, once Mikkel sailed for Greenland they said no more. At times Devin seemed like the friend Mikkel's favorite brother had once been. But that brother had died at sea. And Bree—always Bree stayed just a bit apart.

Why didn't I set her free? Just let her go? Mikkel asked himself. *Free to go back to Tully, whoever he is. Let Bree marry a good Irishman and live happily ever after.*

But deep in his heart Mikkel knew he couldn't just let Bree go. He wanted her to stay on the *Conquest*. Stay in Aurland when they returned home.

Even more, Mikkel hoped that Bree would come to the place where she *wanted* to stay. By now Mikkel wondered if that would ever happen.

For a time he followed Leif easily. Then Mikkel discovered what the tall Greenlander meant by drift ice in the waters between Iceland and Greenland. When Leif swung farther south, Mikkel felt relieved. More than anything, he wanted a safe voyage. Already they had faced enough problems.

Mikkel thought about them. Salt water in the soup. Three men who said they got fresh water from a stream. *Three men I trust.*

Then Shadow let loose, free to escape into the king's house. Bree insisted that she had tied the dog securely. Who wanted to bring harm by letting the dog go? And what did his father know about possible danger to Bree? When Sigurd did not explain, Mikkel felt sure that he had good reason.

But worst of all, the logs cut loose. The night before the accident, he had checked the lashings. They were secure and strong against anything that might come—waves, or whales, or bad weather. Yet Mikkel knew without doubt how close his ship had come to capsizing. Sometime during the night someone had tampered with those ropes.

Someone who hates me. Someone who wants revenge. Who?

One by one, Mikkel started thinking about the men onboard. *Did I make someone angry? Jealous? So upset that he's never forgotten?*

A hundred questions flew around Mikkel's mind. Finally he pushed all of them aside. At the moment he had bigger problems right in front of him. "Our seas are unlike anything you've ever sailed in before," Leif had warned.

Drift ice. Icebergs. Glaciers splitting, ice sliding off the land into the sea.

Not for anything did Mikkel want someone to know how scared he felt. But then he remembered the twenty-five ships led by Erik the Red. *Only fourteen reached Greenland?*

Suddenly Mikkel had still more questions. *What happens when a huge chunk of ice slides into the sea? Is there a mighty splash? A gigantic wave that could flip the* Conquest *over in one moment?*

When Mikkel tried to push his thoughts aside, it was the idea of fog that bothered him most. If there was fog, he wouldn't be able to see anything—not icebergs, not Leif, not even the snow-clad mountain that would keep him from becoming forever lost on the North Atlantic—the ocean that seemed to have no end.

The next morning Mikkel's fear became real. Fog. Fog so thick he could not tell where the water ended and the sky began.

In the stillness of the fog around him—in the muted sound of oars grating in the holes that held them—a thought came to Mikkel.

Maybe this is the place people talk about—the place where people fall off the edge of the earth.

Or maybe it's like the land of the dead that Grandmother feared. Half day, half night, a cold place with freezing fog.

Maybe this is the end of it all—the darkness in which a frightful shape comes to meet us. The darkness in which a hand reaches out like a claw, snatching those who come close.

To Mikkel the gray horror seemed so real that he could not look away from the fog. Standing in the bow of his ship, he peered into the thick mist that hid every sight of what lay ahead.

Mikkel shivered, tried to tell himself he was only cold. But when his right hand rested on the rail, it trembled. Quickly he put his other hand on top of the first. No one must know how frightened he felt.

But he couldn't hide his fear. Not even from himself.

All that day fog surrounded them. When the gray of day blended with the darkness of night, Mikkel only knew that the hours had passed. Whether he was at the bow or tiller, someone brought him food and water. But no one brought him peace.

What if an iceberg lay directly in front of him and he couldn't see it was there? When would a piece of ice hidden below the surface reach up, its sharp edges like a knife, ready to pierce a hole in his ship?

If somehow we manage to live through this voyage—
But what if we do not?

Mikkel knew he had not accomplished the courageous deeds that would bring him into Valhalla, the splendid hall reserved for noble warriors. If he died and wasn't invited there, would he live forever in the place reserved for the old and frail? The place so frightful to Grandmother?

Mikkel wasn't sure, but one thing he knew. He wasn't

willing to take the chance of living this way forever. Whichever way he turned, he felt as if he already lived in that fearful world of the dead.

In Mikkel's heart a cry began. A cry so big that it became the deepest pain he had ever known. *Bree's God. Devin's God. Are You somewhere here with us? Will You help me find the way?*

NINETEEN

THE FLEA

When Bree woke that morning, she knew that something had changed. Each night she set aside a small space for herself—a place on the deck boards between Devin and Nola. There she rolled out her sleeping sack. And there, near the stern of the ship, Bree could often see what was happening.

Now, even before opening her eyes, Bree knew something was wrong. It was too quiet, too still. An eerie stillness.

For a moment Bree lay without moving. Her sealskin sleeping sack kept her warm, but her face and hair felt the dampness. The stillness.

Then Bree opened her eyes and knew. The large sail

hung limp. Fog had settled upon them. A fog so thick that Bree felt she could stir a cooking spoon in its layers.

As she sat up and pulled her cloak over her shoulders, she looked ahead. Only two oarsmen away, the rowers were lost in the fog. Bree could not see beyond them.

Standing at the railing, Bree peered into the fog and found no line of horizon. Only gray mist. Without being told, Bree knew they had lost sight of Leif and his ship.

As panic gripped her, Bree looked for her brother. Wherever he was, Dev was working somewhere in the gray-white cloud that surrounded them.

And then Bree looked for her God. *Fear not* came His words.

But a growing terror edged its way into Bree's mind. *How can I not fear when this voyage was begun without You?*

Fear not? Bree wanted to throw the words back in God's face.

So I'm the one in charge of praying for this ship, she thought bitterly. *But how can I pray in faith? Mikkel planned this trip without asking You about it. How can I seek Your face and cry out to You when I know he wants only honor, and fame, and wealth?*

Sitting down again, Bree leaned forward and buried her face in her lap. When those who had been sleeping started moving around her, she tried to shut them out. Shut out their words, the fear in their voices, the certainty that they would never see land again.

Suddenly Bree understood Thorgeir the Icelander going into his booth and pulling a cloak over his face. Pulling her own cloak over her head, Bree tried to create a space where she only heard God.

Within moments it came. *Do not be afraid, for I have ransomed you.*

The still, small voice that Bree recognized. *I have called you by name; you are Mine.*

With a deep inward sense, God spoke to her panic through words she had memorized. *When you go through deep waters and great trouble, I will be with you. When you go through rivers of difficulty, you will not drown!*

In the hours that followed, Bree lost track of time. But she clung to the words that gave her hope. *For I am the Lord, your God, the Holy One of Israel, your Savior.*

❋

On what Bree thought must be the third day of fog, Devin joined her between two barrels of water and a keg of fish. Whenever possible, they had talked and prayed together. But now, with Devin next to her, Bree once again huddled beneath her cloak.

There Bree heard someone speak her name. This time it was a human voice. "Bree—"

Mikkel. If there was anyone she didn't want to talk with, it was Mikkel.

"Bree—" came the voice again.

Pushing back her cloak, she looked up into Mikkel's face. In the gray mist, his blond hair hung without life around his face. His eyes were wide and dark. The fear Bree saw within them seemed to invade the deepest part of his being.

"Bree? I need your help."

Bree swallowed hard. Unable to speak beyond the lump in her throat, she could only stare at him. *My help? How could she help someone else when she couldn't even help herself?*

Then Mikkel noticed her brother. "Dev?"

Droplets of water lay on the sealskin her brother had thrown over his shoulders. As Mikkel spoke, Devin moved closer.

Kneeling on the deck between them, Mikkel spoke in a quiet and desperate voice. "I want to pray to your God, but I don't know how."

"Pray for safety, you mean?" Bree had been through this with Mikkel before.

"No. I mean yes. I mean no. That's not what I mean. If I die, I want to go to your Heaven."

Sure that she had heard wrong, Bree stared at him.

"Don't you understand?" Mikkel asked. "I want to pray to your God. I want to ask Him to give me what you have."

Like an unexpected gift, Bree felt the surprise of it. *Mikkel wants to know our God?* She couldn't believe it.

"But how do I do it?" Mikkel asked.

Reaching out, Devin put his hand on top of Mikkel's. "You pray," Devin said. "You talk like you're talking to us."

"But how will I know if He hears me?"

"He will."

"If we hit an iceberg—if this ship goes down—if we're lost in a fog forever, it's my fault. I brought all of you here. I can't carry the thought of what might happen to your families. Can your God carry me?"

Devin grinned. "He likes to do that kind of thing."

"I won't be lost in a fog forever?"

Devin shook his head.

"Then tell me the words to pray. If I live, I need the words that will help me know your God. If I'm going to die, I need to meet Him now."

"Pray to Jesus," Devin said. "He's God's only Son and the one who died for you. Tell Him that you're sorry for all the wrong things you've done."

But Mikkel looked doubtful. "You're sure you want to hear it all?"

When he began praying, he stumbled and stopped. But then his words tumbled out as though he had forgotten every thought but one—the sure knowledge that this was something he must do. And with it, he asked forgiveness for his raid on Ireland.

As the torrent of words ended, Mikkel asked, "Is that enough? I think it's everything."

"That's enough," Devin told him. "Ask Jesus to save you from your sin. To be your Savior from every kind of darkness and fog."

But Mikkel was sobbing so hard that he could not pray. For Bree it was terrible to see him cry. Then she saw something else. God taking all the pride, and pain, and mixed-up feelings that tore Mikkel in every direction. God taking everything that Mikkel wanted to give Him. And God giving His comfort.

When at last Mikkel rubbed his hands over his face, he tried to wipe away any trace of tears. Sitting up again, he looked around.

Outwardly nothing had changed. To Bree the cloud of fog seemed even thicker. The gray water still became one with gray sky. In that world in which all sight had vanished, everything remained too still. But then Mikkel said, "I wonder how Leif is."

On the open sea, his words seemed small and lost, but they surprised Bree. Mikkel was thinking of someone besides himself.

During the next night and day Bree, Devin, and Mikkel met in the stern of the ship often. Mikkel wanted to know more about how to pray. To Bree's surprise he wanted to pray, not just for the *Conquest* and its crew, but for Leif, and anyone else who might be lost in the fog. Only after Mikkel prayed for his friend did he pray for those onboard his own ship.

And then, almost as if he had forgotten about the fog that had brought him to his knees, Mikkel asked God to help him guide his ship.

It was some time later as he stood at the steering board, holding a tiller that seemed useless because no one knew where to go, that Mikkel suddenly laughed.

Is he crazy? Bree wondered.

But Mikkel said, "I know what to do!"

A light filled his eyes, and a confidence Bree hadn't seen since the fog began. When Mikkel picked up Shadow, Bree wondered if the strain had snapped his mind.

Sitting down on his sea chest, Mikkel held the dog on his lap. Carefully spreading the hairs on Shadow's back, Mikkel began searching.

"What are you looking for?" Bree asked.

But Mikkel paid no attention. Still dividing the hairs, he leaned close, and then carefully held something up. "I found one!"

As Mikkel moved, Shadow jumped off his lap. Mikkel stood up. "Gather around!" he told his men. As they all drew close, Mikkel set a very small creature on the tiller.

"A flea?"

As the flea began crawling, a cheer went up. Bree stared at the men, bewildered.

"North!" Mikkel exclaimed, pointing. "A flea always crawls north!"

TWENTY

SNOWCAPPED MOUNTAIN

North it is!" the men called out. "And that's where Greenland should be!"

The men took up their oars. They rowed in thick mist, but rowed with a will. Mikkel set the course, and the men did their best to hold to it.

When Mikkel first saw a stretch of white partway up in the sky, he didn't understand what he was seeing. At first he thought the whiteness was an even thicker fog than the gray mist. *Will the moment ever come when I can see again?*

His hand on the tiller, his eyes burning with weariness, Mikkel stared ahead. Like a bundle of yarn spun by his mother, the mist seemed soft, the world not real. Even the movement of oars seemed muted, strangely quiet. Swirling around the ship, the fog hid the dragonhead, then the men sitting only two sea chests ahead of him.

Hoping to catch one small breath of wind, Mikkel ordered the mast raised. It hung limp and lost like a child without friends.

The mist was swirling now. Just above the water— water so gray that there seemed no break between the fog and the waves—Mikkel saw something else. A slanted line of something dark. Something dark beneath the white he thought was fog.

Hardly daring to breathe, Mikkel stared at the dark line. Soon it became something larger, something spread out. And now the mists were swirling again. Was that really a rising wind?

Above him, the sail moved once, twice. Nearby, Devin looked up and turned to grin at Mikkel. Moments later the sail rippled. For an instant the ripple raced across a corner of the cloth. With a stirring that came on cat's feet, the gray around them grew light. A breeze caught the sail and filled it.

In the next moment, Garth climbed the mast so quickly that it seemed he was running. As he reached the top, the last of the fog vanished. With it came his cry. "Land ho!"

Mikkel needed no shout from the mast, for there, from the deck of the ship, he could also see land. Still far away, but directly ahead, a mountain rose from the water. Capped with snow, it seemed to fill the entire earth. *Greenland!*

When a cheer broke out, Mikkel stood there, unable to lift his hand from the tiller. Unable to raise his voice in a shout. Able only to stand and stare at the sight he thought he would never see.

As tears blurred his sight, Mikkel tried to blink them away. He wanted no man to see, no one to catch his weakness. But then Bree turned. When she smiled at him, Mikkel knew that she knew. To his surprise that felt all right.

As another cheer rose from the crew, it echoed in Mikkel's heart. Suddenly he climbed to the rails. For an instant he balanced. Then with a certainty born from walking the mountain heights, he stepped off onto the nearest oar.

The rower gasped, then clung to the oar to hold it steady. When Mikkel jumped to the next oar, the man was ready. To the third, the fourth, the fifth, the sixth oar, Mikkel leaped. Then, catching the rhythm of it, he leaped from one oar to the other as though dancing.

Soon the oarsmen were sure enough of Mikkel's balance to begin rowing again, and Devin started to sing. The tune was Irish, but the song was that of a mighty warrior. As it soared across the sea, one man grinned, and then another. Relief filling his eyes, Mikkel shouted with laughter.

Devin's song was catching. When the men knew the tune, they began to hum, and their strong voices rang out across the water. Soon they dipped and raised their oars in time to the music. And still, like King Olaf himself, Mikkel leaped back and forth upon the oars.

When Mikkel once again looked forward, the *Conquest* drew close to land.

TWENTY-ONE

ERIK THE RED

As Bree watched, Mikkel took hold of the tiller with a new look in his eyes. Always Bree had known how much he liked to sail. Always she had seen his pride in his ship. But now?

Using the position of the sun as a guide, he sailed the *Conquest* up the west coast of Greenland. Facing forward, he studied the sea as if still thinking about their narrow escape. The entire crew knew how close they had come to being lost forever on the North Atlantic.

Part way up the coast, a great heap of rocks rose from a piece of land jutting out into the sea.

"That's it!" Mikkel declared. "The landmark we need to find our way up Erik's Fjord to Brattahlid."

Near the inner end of the fjord, Erik's large farm was easy to recognize by the number of buildings and the size of the longhouse. Leif's ship lay anchored near the shore.

As Bree and the others followed Mikkel off the ship, a big, long-legged dog raced down the slope. Drawing close to Bree, Shadow stiffened at attention. When the other dog came near, Shadow growled.

Low in his throat, the larger dog growled back. When the dog circled Shadow, Mikkel drew close. "Go home!" he told the large dog.

Waiting, Mikkel stood next to Bree until the dog obeyed. Partway to the house it turned, looking back down at them. "Go home!" Mikkel commanded again.

Then a redheaded girl ran to them. Chattering all the way, she led them to the large house with a grass-covered roof and thick walls built of stone and turf. As a brisk wind blew and the damp air fell upon them, the child brought them inside.

The great hall at Brattahlid was filled with people, including the priest King Olaf sent with Leif. In addition to the cooking fire, people warmed themselves around a long hearth. A man-made channel of running water ended in a small pool in the middle of the room.

Leif's mother, Thjodhild [*Turdhild*] hurried forward to meet them. Leif called out, "Welcome to Greenland!"

Mikkel grinned. "After being lost forever." Gone was his usual swagger. Mikkel just sounded relieved to be there. But then as he straightened, Bree saw the strength that had come to him. Once again he wore the marks of a leader.

Leif clapped him on the shoulder. "I was lost too. It upset me to lose you. Both of us could have ended up most anywhere."

"But we are here," Mikkel answered.

"Come, all of you, join us." There was no mistaking the warmth of Leif's welcome.

Long tables filled the great hall, and soon the women set food before Mikkel and his crew. When everyone had been fed, the talk started again.

The face of Leif's mother shone, as if a light came from inside. But Leif's father, Erik the Red, looked like a storm ready to break.

"You say your new God died on the cross?" he asked Leif. "That this Jesus gets rid of the anger our gods feel when people displease them? No one can do that without offering a sacrifice."

"Jesus *is* the sacrifice," Leif told him. "He died for every one of us."

Leif explained. "When we do wrong things, our sin hurts God. It makes Him sad. But Jesus died so that we can receive forgiveness."

Erik shook his head. "It needs to be a blood sacrifice."

"It was. Jesus shed His blood for me and for you."

"This Jesus *died*, you say?"

"On a cross. And then rose up from the dead."

Erik's red hair and beard stood out as bright as a fire around his face. "No one rises from the dead!"

When Leif tried to explain, the sparks of his father's anger flew into the room. Erik pounded his fist on a table. "Why do you want to leave the gods we have always worshiped?"

Without giving time for Leif to answer, Erik stood up. As he pointed his finger at Leif, Erik's hand shook. "You will call down the anger of our gods!"

Whirling around, Erik started across the large hall. Suddenly he turned. "I refuse to offend my god. With his mighty hammer, Thor defeats my enemies on both land and sea."

Reaching the door, Erik flung it open. When he slammed the door behind him, no one moved. In the large room even the children were silent. Then Leif's mother spoke in a strong and steady voice.

"Thank you, my son, for telling us of your new faith. The moment you came I could see the difference in you—the peace you feel—the way you have changed. I believe in the Jesus you know."

Thjodhild looked to the priest. "Can we go down to the river? I want to be baptized in the name of this Jesus. When my time comes to die, I want everyone to know that I am a Christian—that I am forgiven and am clothed in white."

Mikkel's shipload of timber sold immediately. Watching him, Bree felt glad for something that was honestly earned. But a wounded place within her still held back. What would Mikkel do about the treasure he had taken from Glendalough Monastery? What would he do with the coins stolen from his father's friend?

Strange, Bree thought. *Why can't I find a trace of Mikkel's treasure?* She had never stopped looking for it.

And something else bothered Bree. Mikkel had never learned who caused trouble on the way here. *Spoiled soup. Shadow's rope untied. Logs meant to roll if something set them loose.* What else might happen? What dangers still lurked around them without their knowing?

Now Leif encouraged Mikkel to become a trader who traveled across the oceans of the world. "If you return to Norway and come back with more timber, we'll buy everything you bring. We'll give you trade goods that have great value in Ireland and Norway."

Ireland. Even the name of her country filled Bree with hope.

Soon Thjodhild spoke with gladness of heart about the church she wished to build. But her husband Erik asked, "A church? We have a place to worship Thor. We don't need anything else!"

The next time Thjodhild talked about the church,

Erik pounded both fists on the table. "Woman! You will make our gods angry! Haven't I taught our sons well?"

"Yes, you have taught our sons well," Thjodhild replied. "You have taught them to hunt and fish and live with courage. You have taught them to not be afraid of the dangers that lie in the open sea or the unexplored land."

Erik grinned. "See? You are proud of our three sons."

"I am proud," Thjodhild answered quietly. "I am proud of the men they have become."

Leaning back on his bench, Erik made himself comfortable against the wall. "So why do you want to spoil them with this new teaching? Why do you speak against the gods we have always known? If they hear what you say, we will not get fish from the sea or food from the land."

Thjodhild shook her head. "The gods you serve are ones of darkness; and cold, gray mist; and fear. The God I serve is one of love. He is not trying to get even."

But Erik would hear no more about a God who must be weak. If He showed love to people, He could not possibly be anything but weak. Erik would continue worshiping Thor, the god who had the same red hair and beard as he did. After all, Thor had a powerful hammer he threw whenever he needed to destroy his enemies.

In the days that followed, Bree worked in the kitchen with Leif's mother as she had with Mikkel's mother. Day after day Thjodhild asked questions of Leif and the priest. When she learned that Bree and Devin were Christians, she brought questions to them as well.

Soon Bree found favor with Thjodhild. Though Bree was still a slave, she and the other women slept in one of the rooms leading off the great hall. Often Bree and Thjodhild talked about what it meant to be a follower of Christ.

As the winter winds blew down upon Greenland, covering the fjord with ice and snow, people gathered around the long hearth in Erik's great hall. Many were eager to learn, but one day when the priest spoke to them, Erik lost his temper again. Once again, he stalked out of the house, this time into a cold wind that swept in through the door the minute he opened it.

After her friends and neighbors left, Thjodhild huddled by the fire. As Bree prepared food for the evening meal, Leif sat down next to his mother.

"I didn't mean to bring you hardship," he said. "When King Olaf asked me to bring the message of Christ to our land, I told him, 'It will be difficult to bring it to Greenland.' I knew without doubt what my father believed. I knew what the cost would be to you and to me."

Thjodhild straightened. "If you could do it over again, would you make a different choice?"

Reaching out, Leif took his mother's hand and looked into her eyes. "It is true my father taught me well.

Thor is very important to him. Both of them have red hair and thunder when they speak. But I knew so much about Thor that I wanted someone to fill my emptiness. I found it easy to believe in the Christ who came to earth and is like us."

Thjodhild smiled. "Except He has no sin."

Like a cast-off cloak, her discouragement fell away. Light returned to her eyes. "Yes! Instead of shadowy gods that have no power and make us afraid, our Christ is holy—without sin."

Leif nodded. "And He gives us peace."

❦

Thjodhild started keeping a calendar stick much like one Bree had seen in Norway. On the long, narrow, flat board, she cut a small notch each day, marking summer months on one side and winter months on the other. In that far north country, it was important to plant crops by a certain time, and Thjodhild also wanted to keep track of special worship days.

Bree knew the Irish system of telling time—a sundial by day and stars by night. While she was still very young her daddy took her outside, pointed to the heavens, and taught her the position of the stars at different times of the night. Though those positions changed with the seasons, Bree had no trouble telling the hour of the night.

Now Bree never lost track of important days such as

Christmas and birthdays. Here she had no high place where she could gaze upon the waters of the Irish Sea. But during the few moments when she was free of work, she walked to the fjord and watched the water that changed with the seasons.

In summer Bree especially missed the trees of Ireland and their many shades of green. At the fjord near Brattahlid, she met her brother. When she asked, "Do you think Mam and Daddy are worried about us?" Devin smiled.

"They will know."

"Know what?"

"That we are all right. They will pray, and God will give them peace."

From then on Bree felt better. But her thoughts kept going back to Ireland and her family. More often than she liked she thought of Tully.

As Christmas drew near, she wondered, *If I were in Ireland would I receive a special gift from him? And what would I give to Mam and Daddy? My brothers and sisters?*

"Devin," she said, the next time they met by the fjord. "If you were in our mountains, how would you celebrate Christmas this year?"

A grin filled his face, just thinking about it. "On cold nights I would sit around the fire and spin a tale for Keely, Adam, Cara, and Jen. When the sun breaks through and the evenings are soft with the mists of Ireland, I would

find a stretch of green and dance with one such as you—
but one who is *not* my sister."

Bree giggled. "When you return home you will wed
your true love. But who is she?"

"I don't know," Devin said, and a longing for Ireland
was in his eyes. "But I will find her."

"And what would you give your true love for
Christmas?" Bree asked.

TWENTY-TWO

FLOWERS ABOVE THE SNOW

Devin's grin faded. His eyes were on the snow-capped peaks when he answered. "All that I am because I have known this long journey."

There it was. "This long journey." Bree looked at her brother and knew he had grown up. "We need to make this journey count," she said. "When you took Keely home—"

Devin faced her, waiting.

"God reminded me that He asked me to be a light to the nations. It's not just me that He called. God has a reason for both of us being here. Some reason much bigger than us."

"Maybe it's Mikkel," Devin said.

Then Bree remembered. Last Christmas she had asked him, "Do you think Mikkel will ever change?" Her brother grinned and said, "If he has the right friends." Now Bree told him, "You have been the right friend."

"I hope so," Devin answered. "What do you suppose Mikkel will be someday?"

Bree smiled. Sometimes she wondered too. Straight and strong with flyaway hair, skin bronzed by sun and wind, and eyes that looked far across the sea—

But what was happening inside, in the places where she and Devin couldn't see? Was Mikkel changing, growing in the spiritual promises he made when lost in the fog?

Always Bree stayed apart, waiting. In her mind there were too many questions left unanswered.

That evening she began making a Christmas gift for Leif's mother. Because she could not give her own mother a gift, Bree wanted to honor another mother.

At first Bree's fingers felt stiff as she worked with the slender piece of bone that was her needle. Back and forth, back and forth, she pushed the needle through a small piece of cloth she had woven when Thjodhild was outside. Carefully Bree created a design sewed with a thread made red by the juice of summer berries.

On Christmas morning when Bree set the table for the early day meal she placed her gift next to Thjodhild's wooden bowl and spoon.

"What is this?" Leif's mother asked when she saw it. Taking the cloth, she held it up to the light.

The stitching made a picture. An X formed the shape of a manger with bits of straw spilling over the side. A small half circle became the head of a baby. Thjodhild knew at once that it was the Christ child.

"A remembrance," Bree said softly. "A remembrance of the Jesus you serve."

"Ahhh—" Thjodhild smoothed the cloth with her hand, touched the head of the baby with reverence. "This *will* be my remembrance of my first Christmas of knowing Him."

Thjodhild carried it closer to the light of the fire, then looked back to Bree. "My remembrance, both of the Christ I serve and the way you serve me. You do not have to care about me, but I feel that you do."

That day Thjodhild led Bree from the large longhouse. The afternoon was clear and cold, and the sun shimmered on the snow. Bree followed Thjodhild down a narrow path to the edge of a hill.

Below them lay a fold in the land partly hidden by snow. "There I will build a church," Thjodhild said.

"Here?" Bree asked. "This far from your house?"

"Here," Thjodhild said. In the snow she stepped it out. Leaving space between her steps, she set down her feet sixteen times one way and eight times the other. "It will have thick walls of timber and stone to keep out the cold. A steep roof covered with turf, and a small place where I can build a fire to stay warm."

Thjodhild smiled. "Here I will have a church where I can worship the true God."

Standing there, Bree looked down on the fold of land and held Thjodhild's dream in her heart. "The first Christian church in all of Greenland," Bree said.

"Yes!" Thjodhild exclaimed.

Feeling her joy, Bree laughed. And then she knew something more. Leif's mother did not have to build a church. She was not doing it to please an earthly king. Instead, she wanted a place to worship the King of kings who had also become her Lord.

In the spring of the year when ice drifted down the fjord and the river near Erik's house filled with rushing water, the work on Thjodhild's small church began. From Norway to Iceland to Greenland, Leif had carried valuable logs in his ship. Now he, Mikkel, Devin, and several other men took that timber to the site of the church. There they also brought stone and turf.

The small church they built was just as Thjodhild had said—with a bench on the two long sides and a place for a fire. And as Thjodhild wished, the church lay tucked into the fold of land, where her husband, Erik the Red, did not have to look upon it.

With the coming of summer, flowers filled the slope between the house and the fjord. To Bree it seemed there had been no time between the snow and the flowers bursting upon the land. Instead of looking withered and dried from their winter's sleep, they seemed to burst directly from beneath the snow to full bloom.

In the light of the sun, Bree walked among the daisies and angelica and long-stemmed buttercups. But with the summer both Bree and Devin felt impatient to leave.

Here there was no possible way to get home except on a ship leaving from Greenland. In the rare times when a ship came to Erik's Fjord, runners took the message to the surrounding farms. Word of a ship arriving from Norway spread like a wildfire. But Bree always crept close and watched.

Was there a way she and Dev could slip on board and hide until far off at sea? Could she ask to be a cook and earn her way home? But then she saw that Mikkel always set guards around the ships—guards that stayed until the ships left the fjord again.

On the September day that Bree turned fifteen, Mikkel found her walking along the fjord.

"Happy birthday, Bree," he said.

Thanking him, Bree tipped her head and asked, "And when will you take me to Ireland?"

A shadow entered Mikkel's eyes. "I've been gathering more hides and cloth—valuable things to trade."

"But you promised to take Dev and me home at the end of one voyage. Soon you will have so much cargo your ship cannot carry it all."

"This is still one voyage," Mikkel told her.

"Our parents will worry about us. They will think we went down in the sea."

"Don't they know our God protects you?" Mikkel answered.

Bree stared at him, angry at his strange use of truth. *Our God,* Mikkel said. Bree was glad that the faith he held seemed big. With all her heart, Bree believed that his prayer had been real. But there was still too much between them.

Mikkel broke the silence. "Bree, who is Tully?"

The question startled Bree. It had been over a year since Mikkel heard Lil speak of her cousin. Why did Mikkel remember? She didn't want him to enter a part of her world that she felt was special—almost sacred—a part where deep in her heart she cherished Tully as a childhood friend.

Now that she was the age when girls in Ireland often wed, the question hurt Bree even more. Instead of answering, she walked away.

In the winter that followed, Bree knew that Mikkel no longer watched to see if she would try to escape. He knew that she wouldn't, and so did Bree. Where could she go in this country where so much of the land was covered by ice and snow? Even in summer the ice pack on the mountaintops never melted.

As the winds blew cold, people gathered around the long hearth at Brattahlid. While women did their spinning and weaving at one end of the fire, children played nearby. At the other end, men mended their tools and nets and joined in the talk.

More than once they asked Devin to tell them about faraway Ireland. Always he spun his favorite tales, sang Irish songs, played his pipes, and spoke of home. With each telling Bree longed even more to see her family.

That winter everyone talked about Bjarni Herjulfsson. People wondered how he had fared on his trip to Norway. Had he managed the long journey safely? What would King Olaf Tryggvason say about their country? What would Bjarni tell them when he came back?

"And who is Bjarni?" Bree asked.

She learned that as a young merchant, Bjarni spent one winter in Norway and the next with his father in Iceland. When Bjarni returned from one of his trips, he discovered that his father had followed Erik the Red to Greenland. Bjarni set out to follow his father, but was blown off course.

Like Leif and Mikkel, Bjarni was also lost in fog. Missing the southern tip of Greenland, he sailed for days without sight of land. When at last he came upon it, his men wanted to go ashore. But Bjarni said no.

Three times they sighted land. Three times Bjarni said they could not go ashore. They must go on. It was close to winter, and he needed to find his father before the autumn storms set in. Now, fifteen years later, Bjarni had gone to visit the king of Norway.

At Christmas Thjodhild invited people to worship in the new church. Her sons Leif, Thorvald, and Thorstein came, but not their half-sister Freydis. Bree, Devin, a few neighbors, and the priest from Norway crowded inside. Last of all, Mikkel entered the small church.

Thjodhild looked around with a pleased smile on her face. "It is a beginning," she said. "A good beginning."

❀

The fiercely cold months of the winter of 1001–1002 seemed to last even longer than the year before. It was longer still before summer burst upon the land.

Whenever the weather made it possible to travel, Mikkel and Devin went with Leif on missionary trips to other settlements. In one fjord, one settlement, one home after another, Leif told people about his new beliefs and the glory of the God he served. The priest sent by King Olaf went with Leif and baptized the people who believed.

Often Bree heard talk about Leif. "Wise, he is," said many people. "Moderate in all he does. Even tempered."

Even tempered? Sometimes Bree wanted to laugh at

such a description. Didn't Leif ever have a red-hot temper like his father? Yet from all that Bree saw of Leif, she knew the words were true. Manly, sure of himself and the way he wanted to lead, he made strong decisions. Without doubt, Leif had a heart of courage.

Whenever someone spoke of his steady ways, Bree glanced at Thjodhild. As proud as any mother, she seemed to tuck the words away in her heart.

❧

On her sixteenth birthday, Bree walked to the wide plain where Greenland's parliament met. As night faded and dawn slanted across the sky, Bree stood on the shore.

Mikkel found her looking across the fjord at the snowcapped mountains.

"Happy birthday, Bree," he said.

"Thank you," she answered. "And when will you take me home?"

The shadow that entered Mikkel's eyes spread to his face. Then as though pulling a mask over his feelings, Mikkel spoke. "I want to learn from Leif."

"Learn what?"

"How to be an explorer, trader, merchant. How to live as—" Mikkel broke off, then finished. "How to live as a Christian."

"Yes." Again Bree felt glad. But she had no patience left, and it filled her voice. "You promised one voyage."

"This is still one voyage," Mikkel said.

"I am sixteen today!" Bree cried out. "I am growing old waiting for you to take me home."

"Old?" Mikkel grinned, then stood back. "Oh, yes, I see it now. A wrinkle of worry between your pretty eyebrows. It will ruin how you look. You are indeed old."

But Bree felt angry at how the years were slipping away. Years when she wanted to be with her friends. When she wanted to enjoy being a chieftain's daughter.

"In Ireland I will be past the marrying age," she said.

"Really?" Mikkel asked, as if learning something new. But Bree felt sure he already knew the marriage customs of Ireland.

In the next moment Mikkel turned serious. "Bree, who is Tully?"

When Bree met his gaze, she could not answer. She could only wonder if Mikkel heard the pounding of her heart. *Does Tully even remember me?*

Three years had passed since the Viking ship stole Bree away from Ireland. *How can Tully possibly wait for me to come home? He doesn't even know if I'm alive.*

As if realizing he had walked into a place where Bree did not want him to go, Mikkel said, "You don't want to talk about it, do you?"

"I can't," Bree said. "It hurts too much."

Mikkel reached out his hand, but she refused to take it. "When you can talk about it, I'd like to know," he said.

When Devin found Bree walking along the fjord, she was still so upset she could barely speak.

"Why does Mikkel ask about my life? My friends? Why doesn't he just take us home?"

LEIF ERIKSON'S SHIP

As Bree fell into step beside Devin, he said, "Mikkel has changed."

That hurt Bree even more. "The only thing that has changed is that now you're taking his side!"

When Devin was silent, Bree spilled out her anger. "Mikkel says he wants to be a merchant. To be a merchant, he must bring trade goods to other lands. So why does he stay here? For someone who usually puts money first, why is he acting so strange?"

Up and down the shore, Bree paced. Finally she stopped, her gaze on the mountains across the fjord. In the transparent air she felt as if she could reach out and touch them. But Bree was truly angry now. "Why don't his men complain?"

"Only Garth is married, and he has Nola with him."

"So what are all of them doing?" Bree knew that Devin had been working as a blacksmith. But what about the other men?

"Hunting. Finding land for themselves. Gathering pelts and skins. Blubber."

"Blubber?"

Devin grinned. "Fat. You know. Whale oil." But then a thoughtful look entered his eyes. Bree caught it.

"So what do you know that I don't? Why is Mikkel waiting? Why does he stay here?"

"I think something has become more important to him than money." But Devin would not say another word.

As the days of autumn edged toward another winter, Bjarni returned from Norway. With him came word of all that had happened. In September of the year 1000, only a few months after Leif and Mikkel left Nidaros, King Olaf Tryggvason died in battle and Earl Erik became ruler.

When Bjarni told about the lands he had sighted, everyone wanted to know more. "Why didn't you explore the land?" they asked. Soon they decided Bjarni was a man without much curiosity. For hadn't he seen the new lands and never stepped foot on them?

Though honored by the ruling earl, Bjarni felt the

criticism. When he returned home, he brought the Earl's encouragement for further exploration. In Greenland it fell upon ready ears.

That autumn the ice came suddenly. One day the water flowed, the next morning the world was silent and frozen. Often Leif's mother invited others to join her as she worshiped her Lord in the new church. More than once she and Bree tromped down the snow to make a path to the small building.

"If He's full of love, He's weak," Erik scoffed more than once. But now there was something new to talk about around the winter fires. The men spoke of little else but faraway lands.

"What does Bjarni say the land is like?" Mikkel asked during that winter that formed a bridge between 1002 and 1003. Always it was the question that started people talking again.

"How could Bjarni *not* stop there?" Mikkel said to Bree later. "I would want to see every inch of a new land."

For once Bree agreed with him. And Mikkel and Devin agreed about something else—their desire to explore the land Bjarni had seen. Both of them wanted to be among the first Europeans to set foot on that land.

True, time was running out for Bjarni and his men. "The autumn storms were close at hand," Bjarni had said in his own defense. "I needed to find my father while I could."

Around the fire the men nodded. They, too, understood the storms on the oceans of the world.

Then as Bree left the house one morning, she heard the singing of the birds. By now she knew how short a Greenland summer could be. On this day, the beginning of her third spring at Brattahlid, she lingered outside, wanting to feel the warmth of the sun. If she stood there long enough, perhaps the flowers would leap above the last of the snow.

In the clear light above the fjord, the sun caught the drift ice floating downstream. White and silver, pale green filled with light, it shimmered with beauty.

That evening Leif said, "Tomorrow I will visit Bjarni." It wasn't hard to guess what Leif and Bjarni would talk about.

"Can Dev and I go along?" Mikkel asked quickly. The next morning they were among the men chosen to travel to Bjarni's farm on the southwestern coast of Greenland.

When they returned, Leif sailed into Erik's Fjord in a large merchant ship he had purchased from Bjarni. Everyone hurried down to the water to look.

With a high curved prow and stern, the ship had one mast and a large single sail. At the center was a large space that was open down to the ribs of the ship. Into that space Erik and his men would load cargo—provisions that would last for some time.

Though Mikkel's *Conquest* was much smaller, it had

space for many more oarsmen. An ocean-going trading ship called a *knorr*, Leif's ship had places for only twelve oarsmen. Six men sat at the front, with three on one side of the prow and three on the other side. The remaining six men rowed in the area back of the cargo. The ship also carried a small boat for going ashore.

"Come with us," Leif asked his father as he showed Erik the ship.

"No, no, I am too old."

But Leif asked again. "Please be leader of our voyage. You know more than any of us about exploring new lands."

"But my bones are stiff. I cannot stand wet and cold weather as I did when I was young."

"Of all our relatives you would be the best leader."

Again Erik shook his head.

Each day Thjodhild and the other women prepared provisions for the thirty-five men Leif planned to take along. By now Bree knew exactly what to do to get ready for a voyage. Each time she brought more supplies to the ship, she looked at its strong timbers, imagined the sail filling with wind, and felt the spray of salt water in her face. Always she wondered, *Will I be allowed to go?*

No longer did she want to stay behind. No longer did her fear of what might happen bring a quaking in her spirit that unsettled her nights and her days. Instead she asked herself, *What if Dev and Mikkel go, and I'm left behind?*

Like the two boys, Bree longed to be chosen for the voyage to unknown lands. Each time they talked about it, Bree felt an excitement in her heart.

"Leif will only take men," Mikkel said one day. "Thirty-five men, he says."

"He won't take women along?" Bree asked. "Who will do the work?"

Mikkel stared at her. "You want to go. Briana O'Toole, the Irish lass who says she wants to go home? Now you want to become an explorer?"

"I'm not a lass. I'm a colleen."

By now Mikkel had learned that *lass* was a Scottish word. Just the same, he called Bree a lass whenever he wanted to tease her.

The minute he saw Devin, Mikkel asked, "Do you know what your sister said?" He told him.

Devin's eyes filled with laughter. "Good," he told Bree. "I didn't want to leave you behind."

One day, as she watched Leif prepare for his voyage of exploration, Bree thought about the peace that had come to Brattahlid. All through their travels from the Aurland Fjord to Greenland, things had gone wrong.

The salty water that spoiled the fish soup. Shadow let off his rope to find a way into the king's house. Logs cut loose, nearly causing Mikkel's ship to capsize.

Who tried to hurt Mikkel? Bree wondered. What man in his crew has remained silent all this time? Silent and waiting? The more Bree thought about it, the more it worried her.

Waiting for what? Bree asked herself. *Why do I keep wondering if something will happen to Mikkel? Does someone still want to get even? If so, why?*

As often as she disagreed with Mikkel, Bree didn't want to see him hurt. When she talked to Devin about it, he agreed.

"You're right, Bree, it's really strange. Maybe there's something that person wants before he gets revenge."

"Something like stolen treasure?" Bree asked.

Devin nodded, but said no more.

Yet in spite of her questions about danger to Mikkel, Bree felt peace in Erik's house. In spite of his fiery temper. In spite of all the talk that swirled around his home. Talk of new lands and new adventure. Talk of exploration of a world that those with hearts of courage wanted to see. And Leif led them all in their thinking.

Would there be a longer summer in those lands? Less snow and ice? Trees, more land for animals to graze, a warmer climate for food to grow?

Whenever Bree felt excited about Leif's voyage, she also had questions. *Will the person who wants to hurt Mikkel be along? If he is, what will happen?*

As Bree worked around the house, she heard Erik the Red talk about what troubled him. "Why do you want to draw settlers away from Greenland?" he asked Leif.

"I don't." Leif sounded as if it had never occurred to him.

"But if you find a good land, you will."

"It would be many years—" Leif started to explain. "First we need to find Bjarni's land. Then we need to explore it. To set out with ships and people, animals, and seed, and supplies—"

When Leif stopped, Bree knew he had seen the anger in his father. "We need you to lead us," Leif said quietly. "You are the most experienced among us."

But Erik answered, "Take your foster father, Tyrker the Southerner. And the Scottish couple King Olaf gave you. If you need someone to run fast—someone to explore new land—they can do it."

"But you?" Leif asked. Again he encouraged his father to go along.

Finally Erik agreed.

TWENTY-FOUR

MORE THAN A VOYAGE

Mikkel's questions kept coming back to one thought: *Why didn't Bjarni go ashore on the lands he saw?*

True, he needed to find Greenland before winter. Anyone who lived in the North understood the fury of autumn storms. But now a fire burned in Mikkel's heart. *I want to see the new land. I want to set foot on that shore where no European has stepped before.*

Once or twice Mikkel thought of the fame he would gain and perhaps the wealth. Then, to his own surprise, he realized there was something he cared about more. Bree, and Devin, and others in his life. And deep in his bones, Mikkel wanted to explore new land and discover a good place for people to live.

When Mikkel realized that, everything else fell away. No longer did the gems and coins he had secretly brought on his ship seem important. What did that mean when compared with seeing a new world?

Then, as he thought about the treasure, Mikkel knew. Like a flash it came to him. *The man who wants to get even. The man who hates me so much that he wants revenge.* And Mikkel knew why.

He wanted to lead the raid on the monastery at Glendalough. And I said no. I said he must guard the ship.

As though it happened yesterday, Mikkel remembered. *I wanted the gems, the treasures, the wealth. But I didn't want people hurt.*

During the raid, he had bargained with Brother Cronan. Unknown to Mikkel, the monk was both teacher and friend to Devin and Bree. When Mikkel threatened him, Brother Cronan traded a holy book covered with gems for the safety of his people. *And I was glad for the bargain!*

Now Mikkel could only feel humble with the certain knowledge that God had kept him from killing someone. But the man who wanted to lead the raid?

He still wants the wealth that I gained. He thinks I stood in his way and wants revenge. But I can't prove it. I can't prove he cut the ropes in the ship—that he put all of us in danger.

From that day on, Mikkel knew he needed to be continually on guard.

From that time on, he also did his best to make

himself valuable to Leif. Wasn't he, Mikkel, skillful as a swordsman? An excellent man with bow and arrow? The experienced master of a ship? Hadn't he already found his way through the fogs of Greenland? If he was to return with logs for this treeless land, he needed to know everything he could about the surrounding seas.

When Leif chose him for the voyage, Mikkel felt relieved. Then he tried to be sure that Devin and Bree would be asked to go.

One after another, Leif chose the men he wanted, offering a share of the profit to each person who agreed to go along. Whenever a new man was chosen, Mikkel and Devin added up the count. There were fewer and fewer places left to fill.

"Dev is a really good blacksmith," Mikkel told Leif as they worked side by side. Hearing his own words, Mikkel wondered when he had started using Bree's name for her brother.

"You're certain about that?" Leif asked. As if he hadn't taken the words to mind, Leif continued loading his ship.

"As certain as the sun rises and sets. Look at the rivets on my ship. Devin made them on our forge in Aurland. Don't forget he's a storyteller too. And he plays the pipes."

Leif broke out in laughter. "I've lost count of the

times you've told me. And Bree? I suppose you will speak of her again, too?"

When Leif chose the next man, it was Devin. He and Mikkel could hardly wait to tell Bree. Acting as though it wasn't really important, they walked from the fjord at their usual pace. But when they came into the large open room in Erik's longhouse, Devin hurried over to Bree. "He asked me!"

Bree stiffened. "Leif?" she asked.

"I'm the thirty-fifth man chosen to go!"

Seeing the stillness in Bree's face, Mikkel poked Devin. "Come here," he said. Leaving Bree behind, he led Devin outside.

"We have to pray," Mikkel said, surprising even himself. "We can't leave Bree here alone."

TWENTY-FIVE

DANGER, DANGER!

That afternoon Bree prepared the meal she knew to be Leif's favorite. With precious honey imported from Norway, she made oatcakes. For the one-hundredth time she prayed desperately that she would be allowed to go. So far she knew of only one other woman who had been asked—the Scottish woman who could run as fast as a deer.

As Bree set the special food before him, Leif spoke to her. "Mikkel tells me you're a good cook."

"Oh?" Surprised, Bree glanced toward Mikkel. He had seldom told her.

"I've told Nola I want her to go—"

Bree turned away, trying to hide her disappointment.

Nola was a good friend, and Leif had chosen rightly. Though Bree didn't want to admit it, Nola was a better cook.

But then Leif's voice stopped Bree. "Nola says she needs your help."

When Bree looked into Leif's eyes, she knew he was teasing her. Then, looking beyond Leif, Bree saw the gladness in Mikkel's face.

Drawing herself up, Bree stood with dignity before this leader she respected. "Yes," she said, her voice stronger than she felt. "It's important that you have thirty-five men, but also three women."

The next day the wind blew fair, and Leif said, "Tonight we will finish loading. In the morning we will leave."

That afternoon and into the twilight before complete darkness, Bree packed whatever was needed. Some of the barrels for dried fish were large and would have to be carried by men. Others were smaller kegs that Bree recognized from Mikkel's ship. As she finished packing the last keg, she noticed a special mark on the side.

Bree knew that gash on one of the staves. She remembered how it came about. That long-ago day when she entered the boathouse, Mikkel had quickly covered something. Then, as he worked on a narrow strip of wood to make a stave, his ax slipped.

Later that day Bree had returned to the boathouse,

hoping to find out what Mikkel hid. But the table had been empty. The nearby shelves held only tools.

Now Bree set the lid in place, picked up the keg, and started toward Leif's ship. She was nearly there when she felt one of the staves move. When she set the keg in the cargo hold, the stave moved again.

Suddenly Bree knelt down and ran her hand over the narrow piece of wood. During their three years in Greenland, the wood had dried and the stave fit more loosely. As though tracing a wound, Bree's finger followed the gash, still feeling Mikkel's anger.

To her surprise the stave moved slightly upward. When Bree pushed at the gash, the wood slid far enough open to show a space at the bottom of the keg.

Standing up, Bree glanced around. *No one in sight.*

Then a shadow moved along the side of a nearby ship. Bree waited, watching, but couldn't be sure if someone was there. She could be certain, though, that someone stood up the slope near the house where it was lighter.

Far enough, Bree thought, feeling relieved. If she didn't search now, she might never get the chance. Kneeling again, she slipped her hand into the opening. A hollow space lay between the bottom of the keg and a thin piece of wood above.

Feeling around inside the space, Bree found a small leather bag. Drawing it out, she set it on the deck. Searching again, she found a second, then a third bag.

Ah! One by one, she held up the bags in the dusky light. The first had no mark whatsoever. Just a plain leather bag, heavy and lumpy with coins. Bree felt sure that Mikkel had earned them in honest trade.

The second bag? In the leather Bree saw the mark of a bear, just as Devin had described. When she opened the bag, she found gold and silver coins. Most had a design she didn't recognize. Without doubt they were the coins stolen from Bjorn the cobbler, the friend of Mikkel's father.

Hurrying now, Bree shoved the first and second bags back into the secret place and picked up the third. When she untied the cord at the top, she let the contents spill out onto the palm of her hand.

Gems! Beautiful gems, even in the dim light. Bree had no doubt that they were jewels of great value. There was only one place from which those gems could have come. Glendalough! For many years pilgrims had brought valuable gifts to the monastery. Often the monks used them on the covers of the Bibles they copied by hand.

Filled with awe, Bree barely heard a dog bark, then voices. In that instant she remembered the danger of someone finding her. Moving quickly, Bree held the third bag open. Tipping her hand, she dropped the gems inside. But some of them spilled over, fell to the deck, and rolled.

Heart racing, Bree searched for the gems. One by one,

she dropped them into the bag. As the voices drew closer, she tied the top, pushed the bag into the open space, and closed the stave.

Standing up, Bree rolled the keg over next to the others. Filled with relief, she set it in place.

Just then she heard a sound behind her. Whirling around, she saw Mikkel standing there, his face filled with anger.

"So, you found them?" he asked.

"Found what?" Bree tried to pretend she didn't know.

"You know what I'm talking about. The coins and gems that made me a wealthy fourteen-year-old."

"So? What about them?" With all her willpower Bree kept herself from turning to look at the keg.

But Mikkel walked over and tipped it on its end. "Well, at least you got the stave closed right."

"The stave?" Bree still acted innocent.

But her words increased Mikkel's anger. Deliberately, as if he had all the time in the world, Mikkel set the keg in place. When he straightened again, he faced her.

"What did you find?"

When Bree did not speak, his words lashed out again. "What did you find?"

As Bree started to tremble, she remembered Dev's long-ago words. *If Mikkel knows that you know he stole from his father's friend, he'll never let you go back to Ireland.*

Slowly, deliberately, Mikkel took out his dagger.

When Bree gasped, he knelt down. Using the point of the knife, he pried a gem from where it had lodged between two boards.

When Mikkel picked up the gem, he held it between his thumb and forefinger. Without saying a word, he held the gem in front of Bree's face.

Like a stream at floodtide, thoughts tumbled through her mind. *Not go home to Ireland?* Then, as sure as Bree stood there, she knew something else. *Not go on Leif's voyage.*

Her gaze on the gem, she could only think of its great value. *Value?* In that moment Bree wanted to laugh in Mikkel's face. The gem seemed a symbol of the three years she had spent as a slave. A slave in bondage to coins and gems hidden in a wooden keg. A slave in bondage to Mikkel's greed.

Bree straightened, but thoughts still tumbled through her mind. *I thought Mikkel had changed, but has he? I can't let him get by with this.*

Like a cry in the darkest night, Bree prayed without moving her lips. Then with head high and gaze steady, she faced him. "You stole those gems. They're a symbol of your greed."

As though she had struck him, Mikkel stepped back. When he answered, he spit out his words. "My wealth, you mean."

Bree shook her head. "No. That wooden keg holds

what you think is wealth, but it can hurt you more than anything you know."

Mikkel straightened, standing inches taller than Bree. "I'll take care of the treasure."

"And how will you take care of it?"

"It's not your worry."

"Not my worry?" Bree's anger spilled out of control. "It's the Irish you robbed. My people. It's your honesty that's involved if—"

Bree stopped. As angry as she was, she didn't want to say it.

Mikkel stared at her. "After all this time, do you doubt what I believe?"

Now Bree felt she was running for her life. When she spoke again, her voice was little more than a whisper. "Mikkel, would you sell your soul for wealth and fame?"

As though she had struck him, Mikkel stepped back. "Thanks, Bree. I thought we were starting to be friends. That you had learned to trust me."

Feeling as if her life was unraveling again, Bree stared at him. "How can I trust you if I wonder whether you'll be honest?"

Turning, she started away. *I've lost everything,* she told herself. *Everything I really care about. Going on Leif's voyage. Going home. Becoming free.*

But then Bree knew something else. How could she have remained silent and still live with herself? How could she and Mikkel ever be friends if his dark secret lay between them?

As Bree hurried off the ship, she saw a shadow again. This time it seemed to melt into a shed near the water. This time the shadow seemed to take a familiar shape. Did one of the twins watch from there? Was it Garth or Hammer making sure she was all right?

Whoever it was, he was lurking for some reason of his own. Bree felt certain that he, too, had learned about Mikkel's hidden treasure.

For the rest of the night Bree lay awake. In the darkness of her fear God seemed far away. Would she be allowed to go on Leif's voyage? Or would Mikkel tell him that she should stay in Greenland?

When the new day dawned the wind blew fair, and Leif's men carried the last barrel of water on board. Bree stood near the house, hoping she wouldn't be noticed. Maybe she could just slip on board at the last moment. As she waited to see what would happen, Bree offered a prayer filled with pain. *Jesus, I need Your heart of courage.*

When it was time to leave, Erik came outside and said good-bye to Thjodhild. His legs were stiff as he climbed on his horse and set out toward the ship.

Though the distance was not far, Leif rode another horse slowly, staying next to his father. Walking behind them, Bree watched Erik.

Even now, she understood little about this man who

had been outlawed from Iceland. Forced to leave wife, children, and friends behind, Erik had sailed into unknown waters. Yet he had discovered this land and led settlers here.

Now, beneath the hooves of Erik's horse lay the soft green grass of his farm. Like an oasis in a land filled with ice, the grass spread out, rich with color. As he rode, Erik glanced up and down the waterway, then across the fjord to the mountains.

After one more look around, Erik faced ahead, as though preparing himself to leave the place he loved. In that moment his horse stumbled. Erik flew off, landing hard upon the ground.

Leif was the first to reach him. "Here, let me help you up." But when he tried to stand, Erik could not put his weight on one foot.

"I cannot go like this," he said. "If I go on a voyage, I must be well and strong."

"You can still lead us," Leif answered. "We'll do the heavy work."

But Erik shook his head. "It is not fated that I shall discover more lands than this green land on which we live. This will be the end of our traveling together."

As Leif stood there, the sadness he felt showed in his face. Clearly he did not want to leave his father. Nor did he want to be separated from him because they had chosen different paths in what they believed. But then Erik told him, "You must go without me."

For a moment longer Leif waited, looking into his father's eyes. Then, as though knowing he had no choice, Leif helped his father onto his horse. As Erik started back to the house, Leif watched him go.

When Leif turned toward the fjord, his face still showed his disappointment. Then he looked up at the tall mast. At the very top flew his banner.

In that moment Leif threw back his shoulders. As he gave the command, he stood straight, and strong, and tall. "Prepare to leave!"

Every man bent to his work. In the scurry around the ship, Bree and the dog Shadow slipped on board.

When the large merchant ship sailed away from Brattahlid, Leif's mother stood on a stretch of green grass. When she raised her hand in farewell, the light of encouragement shone in her face. But Leif's father, Erik the Red, was nowhere in sight.

TWENTY-SIX

THE DEW OF HEAVEN

As Bree watched the growing distance between Erik's farm and Leif's ship, she felt as if she was holding her breath. Hunkering down between two barrels, she made herself as small as possible. Could it possibly be that after her argument with Mikkel she would be allowed to stay with the voyage? Or had Mikkel just not noticed her?

Seated near the bow of the ship, he and Devin leaned forward, back, forward, back, rowing with all their might. With each dip of their oars, the twelve men worked together. On the starboard, or steering board side, Leif stood at the tiller, guiding the large trading ship. High overhead, at the top of the great mast, his banner rippled in the breeze. Wind filled the majestic sail.

When the ship reached the end of Erik's Fjord, Leif turned into the Davis Strait. Following Bjarni's directions, he headed north. Staying well out from the jagged shoreline, he sailed up the west coast of Greenland.

Only then did Bree believe that she would not be sent back. For the first time since her argument with Mikkel she started to think clearly. After spitting out her anger, she had spent the night feeling sure Mikkel would talk to Leif. Now, through that fear, came two comforting thoughts. *I wasn't left behind, after all. And I didn't tell Mikkel that I know he stole from his father's friend.*

But then Bree remembered the shadow of someone lurking near Leif's ship. Whoever that person was, he had watched and listened. *Someone knows where the treasure is.*

The thought sent a cold chill down Bree's spine. *Mikkel is in danger again.*

From her place between barrels Bree looked around. It was easy to pick out which of Mikkel's men Leif had chosen for this voyage. One by one, Bree counted them. Six men.

But Nola had told her that Garth wasn't along on Mikkel's trip to Ireland. *Five men, counting Hammer. But would he have gone to Ireland without his twin? Did any of those five men take part in the raid?* Bree felt sure that if she knew that answer, she would know who wanted to get revenge.

After a time, Leif's ship changed direction. As they sailed out across the open sea, Bree struggled to remember the faces of each Viking on the voyage from Ireland. Finally she had to give up. She had been too afraid, too seasick, too angry to remember all of them. After three years her memory held the faces of only the tallest and the shortest—those who stood out in some way. Those of average height had faded away.

Two days later Leif found the land that Bjarni and his men had seen last.

When Leif anchored his ship in a sheltered harbor, the men put out the small boat.

Bree edged that way, hoping to go ashore. Instead, Leif took only fighting men and those chosen to row. As Mikkel and Devin took up oars, her brother looked back at Bree and grinned.

The moment the boat reached land, men spilled onto the shore. To Bree's surprise the boat returned. This time she was allowed to go along.

When Shadow followed her into the boat, Bree held him on her lap so he wouldn't take up room. As they drew close to shore, he wiggled loose, leaped over the side, and swam the rest of the way.

On either side of the landing place, trees grew on the slopes. Following a small stream, Leif and the other men started up, climbing along its banks. As Bree followed them, Mikkel fell into step beside her. Bree hadn't talked with him since their last night in Brattahlid. Instead, she had managed to avoid him.

"Bree, I'm sorry about what happened," Mikkel said now. "When I get to Ireland I'll do what's right."

"Will you?" Bree's hurt still went so deep that she could barely speak. "Will you really?" With all her heart she wanted to believe him. With just as much heart she was afraid to try.

"Really. You can trust me. I promise."

Tears welled up in Bree's eyes. "I want to, Mikkel. I want to believe what you say. And I want to believe in you."

As a tear slid down her cheek, Mikkel reached out and gently wiped it away. "I'm learning to pray," he said. "Do you know what I'm asking? For Jesus to give me His heart of courage."

Stunned, Bree stopped, unable to move on. "What did you say?"

When Mikkel repeated his prayer, Bree knew she had to tell him. "That last morning at Brattahlid I asked for the same thing."

Mikkel's smile reached even his eyes. "Thank you, Bree. You didn't need to tell me, and I'm glad that you did."

Taking the hand he offered, Bree let Mikkel help her around the slippery ground near the stream. As they continued climbing, her heart sang. It felt good to have peace between them. Even more, she was glad he was growing spiritually. Then Bree remembered her troubled thoughts.

"Mikkel, which of the men on this voyage went with you to Ireland?"

"Why do you ask?"

"I'm afraid for you."

"Me too." But Mikkel grinned.

"No, I mean it. The man who cut the logs loose— who nearly capsized your ship—why does he want to get even with you? Is he on Leif's ship now?"

But Mikkel wouldn't tell her. "I'm watching my back," he said.

When they reached the top of the hill, Leif and the other men stood on a large open area with neither grass nor trees. Staring at the slabs of rock that stretched far off to ice-capped mountains, Bree remembered the fields of Ireland. She remembered the green grass and the sheep that grazed upon it. Then Leif spoke.

"We won't have it said of us, as it was of Bjarni, that we did not go ashore on this land. I will now give it a name—Helluland."

Around Leif, the men grinned at the meaning of the name—Flat Rock or Stone-slab Land. Such a land was good for nothing.

Glad to be set free, Shadow ran around, sniffing at everything. When Bree and Mikkel started back to the ship, they again walked on the slippery slope close to the stream. Partway down, Bree glanced up and saw a rock slab extending out above them. When Mikkel passed close to the water, Shadow suddenly barked.

Bree stopped. It was Shadow's warning bark. Racing over to Mikkel, he barked again. Again Bree looked up. This time she saw a face on the ledge above them. Just then a rock started to move.

With one shove Bree pushed Mikkel out of the way. As he fell to the ground, the rock crashed on the place he had stood only moments before.

This time it was Bree who stretched out a hand to help him up. As Mikkel took it, his face was white.

When they reached the shore, everyone was waiting. Everyone but one person. Now Bree knew which twin was which. In the moment before Hammer pushed the rock, Bree saw the hate in his eyes.

"What's wrong?" Leif asked as Mikkel and Bree reached the shore. When they told him, Leif said, "We'll wait for Hammer to come."

Mikkel went to Garth. "Your brother—your twin—"

"Hammer is angry," Garth said.

"Yes," Mikkel said. "I know why he hates me. He wants to get even."

Garth nodded. "When I guessed the truth about the logs on the ship, I started watching him. I thought if I watched closely enough, I could keep him from hurting you."

Garth shook his head. "Today that wasn't enough. His thoughts are twisted by hatred."

As Hammer walked out of the trees, men grabbed hold of his arms. When they tied him up, Hammer was silent. But Bree knew that if she could see his eyes, she would always recognize him.

Once again Leif put out to the open sea where it was safer than sailing close to shore. Three days later, they sighted another land, drew close, and cast out the anchor. Again the men rowed ashore in the small boat.

This time Bree stayed on the ship. As far as she could see, the land was level and full of trees. The shore had broad stretches of white sand. Bree wished she could feel the sand between her toes.

Once again Leif looked around. As he spoke, his strong voice reached Bree and the others. "This land shall have a name in keeping with its nature," he said. "I call it Markland."

Forest Land. Leif had named it well. This time his men laughed. Rather than naming the land for what it was not, Erik's son had named the land for what it was.

To take advantage of a wind blowing from the northeast, Leif and his men returned to the ship as quickly as possible. After being out of sight of land for two days, they once again sighted land and sailed toward it. When they drew close, they discovered an island on the north end of the land. There they found shelter on the side away from the wind.

Early the next morning, they climbed to the highest point on the island to look around. As Leif led them, Bree, Mikkel, Devin, and the others fell in behind.

After their days at sea it felt good for Bree to stretch her legs. She felt the warmth of the sun on her face, then the light in her heart. Then she felt Mikkel's gaze rest upon her.

"Bree, the other day—" He stopped, then went on. "If we hadn't walked together—"

"I know," she said. "If I hadn't been willing to trust you—"

When Bree looked at him, Mikkel tried to speak, but could not. Neither could Bree.

The grass was green and plentiful, and the dew sparkled in the morning sun. Dropping to her knees, Bree reached out and wet her fingers.

Water, she thought as she brought her fingers to her mouth. *Fresh, life-giving water!*

Leaning forward again, Bree cupped the grass. When she lifted her hands, the grass fell away, but the water remained.

For a moment Bree looked at the palms of her hands and her fingers wet with the moisture of earth. Still holding her hands like a cup, Bree bowed her head and drank.

Around her, Mikkel and Devin did the same. Farther

off, Leif knelt, drinking the dew of Heaven. Again and again he lowered his hands, filled them with water, and brought them to his mouth. Each time he drank, he looked up.

When at last they all stood to leave, they agreed that they had never before tasted anything so sweet.

As they started down the hill, Bree took a long, deep breath. *What's next?* she wondered. Whatever it was, she felt sure it would be good.

ACKNOWLEDGMENTS

When Jesus walked on earth He told us about a man who cared. Jesus did not give us the man's name —only his country of Samaria and a window into his character. Yet through the ages and throughout the world we have remembered that man as the Good Samaritan.

Not only did the Good Samaritan give first aid to the man who was robbed and beaten, and fell by the wayside. He took the injured man to a safe place, arranged ongoing care, and shared his resources to make the right things happen. The Good Samaritan gave of his time and of his heart.

I would not be able to write a novel such as this without the help of countless individuals who gave both time and heart. I'm grateful to each of these people:

In Norway:

At the Local History Center in Aurland:

Anders Ohnstad, historian, author, and teacher; Ingvar Vikesland, able communicator, teacher and headmaster, now principal; Frazier LaForce, teacher and local cultural consultant.

The Bergen Maritime Museum, Bergen, and Captain Bjørn Ols'en, retired, volunteer; Trondheim Aktivum AS, Trondheim, for help with the city as it was in the King Olaf Tryggvason time period.

In Northern Ireland:

Elaine Roub, faithful encourager and provider of details.

In the Republic of Ireland:

Dr. Felicity Devlin, Education Officer, Education and Outreach Department, National Museum of Ireland, Dublin; Christopher Stacey, Mountain Leader, Footfalls Walking Holidays, County Wicklow, www.walkinghikingireland.com.

In the United States:

Millie Ohnstad, heritage tour leader and genealogical editor of *Aurland Newsletter, Past and Present;* Dr. Bjorn Hurlen, Lake Region Family Chiropractic Clinic, and former resident of Bergen; Dean Sather, Executive Director, Heritage Hjemkomst Interpretive Center,

Moorhead, MN; Thomas Pedersen, Viking resource person; Dr. John Robert Christianson, Research Professor of History, Luther College, Decorah, Iowa; Vicki Palmquist, founder, Children's Literature Network, www.childrensliteraturenetwork.org.

Charlotte Adelsperger; Robert and Rhonda Elmer; B. J. Hoff; Janette Oke; Ken Gire; the ChiLibris authors; Andy Olsen; Al and Mary Lou Olsen; Dagan and Kay Lisenbee.

Judy Werness; Nadine Floren; Robin Thompson; Cindy Giroux; Linda Kusmak; Dorothy and Alan Langstaff; Steve and Judy Eng, Jenny and Matthew; David and Anne Gran; Sue and Steve Davidson; Chuck and Dee Brown; Fred and Sarah Townsend; Jeff and Cynthia Johnson, Daniel, Justin, and Jennifer; Kevin and Lyn Johnson, Nate, Karin, and Elise; my Thursday morning group; my long-time friends and encouragers.

My agent, Lee Hough, and Alive Communications; Barbara LeVan Fisher for her cover design and logo; Greg Call for his cover illustration and inside art.

The great folks at Moody: Dave DeWit, Andy McGuire; Cessandra Dillon; Amy Peterson; Lori Wenzinger; Pam Pugh; Carolyn McDaniel; John Hinkley; Gene Eble; and the entire team.

My husband, Roy, my awesome idea giver, the friend who encourages me in all kinds of circumstances, and the one I love being with for an amazing number of reasons.

Finally, and most important, I'm grateful to my Lord for caring for me and my loved ones. He also cares deeply about you.

My thanks to each of you who translated the Vinland Sagas and spent years of study to ferret out their secrets. I offer my interpretation of what happened with humility and within the framework of my ever-present need to meet a deadline. I have found the following books and Web site especially helpful:

Åsmund Ohnstad, editor, *Among the Fjords and Mountains: A summary of Aurland's history*, Aurland Historical Association, ©1994.

Byock, Jesse L., *Viking Age Iceland*, Penguin Books, New York, N.Y., ©2001.

Fitzhugh, William W. and Elisabeth I. Ward, editors, *Vikings: The North Atlantic Saga*, Smithsonian Institution Press, Washington and London, in association with the National Museum of Natural History, ©2000 by the Smithsonian Institution.

Haywood, John, *Encyclopaedia of the Viking Age*, Thames and Hudson, Inc., New York, N.Y., ©2000.

Ingstad, Helge, *Land Under the Pole Star*, St. Martin's Press, New York, ©1966.

Joyce, P. W., *A Social History of Ancient Ireland*, vol. 1 & 2, originally published 1903, republished in the U.S., Irish Genealogical Foundation, Kansas City, MO, ©1997.

Konstam, Angus, *Historical Atlas of the Viking World*, Checkmark Books, New York, N.Y., ©2002.

Pohl, Frederick J., *The Viking Settlements of North America*, Clarkson N. Potter, Inc., New York, N.Y., ©1972.

Sturluson, Snorri, *From the Sagas of the Norse Kings*, Dreyers Forlag, Oslo, ©1967.

Thorsson, Ornolfur, *The Sagas of Icelanders*, Viking, Penguin Group, New York, N.Y., Leifur Eiriksson Publishing Ltd., 1997, first published by Viking Penguin, ©2000.

The Viking Network Web site, sponsored by The Nordic Council of Ministers, www.viking.no.

Viking Quest Series

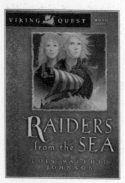

Raiders from the Sea

In one harrowing day, Viking raiders capture Bree and her brother Devin and take them from their home in Ireland. After the young Viking leader Mikkel sets Devin free on the Irish coast, Bree and Devin embark on separate journeys to courage.

ISBN: 0-8024-3112-7
ISBN-13: 978-0-8024-3112-7

Mystery of the Silver Coins

In this second installment of the Viking Quest series, Bree finds herself in a physical and spiritual battle for survival in the homeland of her Viking captors. Bree must face her unwillingness to forgive the Vikings, and Mikkel, the Viking leader who captured Bree, begins to wonder: Is the god of these Irish Christians really more powerful than our own Viking gods?

ISBN: 0-8024-3113-5
ISBN-13: 978-0-8024-3113-4

The Invisible Friend

In this novel, Bree arrives in Norway and is sent to work as a slave for the family of Mikkel, her young Viking captor. She struggles to adjust to the life of a slave, feeling worthless and disrespected, and asking God why He wants her in Norway. As God answers her prayers, Bree faces an important question: No matter who we are or where we live, what does it mean to be truly free?

ISBN: 0-8024-3114-3
ISBN-13: 978-0-8024-3114-1

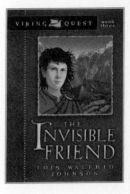

After spending years in Greenland, Bree, her brother Devin, and the Norwegian Viking, Mikkel enter a new world with the explorer, Leif Erikson. First they decide to build a shelter for winter survival. But then how do they protect the ship that is their only hope for returning home? Danger is always lurking. Will Mikkel keep his promise to Bree and Devin and take them home to Ireland? What if keeping a promise becomes a matter of life or death?

ISBN: 0-8024-3116-X
ISBN-13: 978-0-8024-3116-5

Coming in
Early 2006 . . .

*Viking Quest
Book #5*

The last book
in the series!

HEART OF COURAGE TEAM

ACQUIRING EDITOR
Andy McGuire

BACK COVER COPY
Michele Straubel

COPY EDITOR
Cessandra Dillon

COVER DESIGN
Barb Fisher, LeVan Fisher Design

COVER PHOTO
Greg Call

INTERIOR DESIGN
BlueFrog Design

PRINTING AND BINDING
Bethany Press International

The typeface for the text of this book is
Centaur MT